THE WORKS OF ANATOLE FRANCE
IN AN ENGLISH TRANSLATION
EDITED BY FREDERIC CHAPMAN

MOTHER OF PEARL

MOTHER OF PEARL
BY ANATOLE FRANCE
A TRANSLATION BY
FREDERIC CHAPMAN

Fredonia Books
Amsterdam, The Netherlands

Mother of Pearl

by
Anatole France

ISBN: 1-4101-0516-4

Fredonia Books
Amsterdam, The Netherlands
http://www.fredoniabooks.com

CONTENTS

CONTENTS

THE PROCURATOR OF JUDÆA

MOTHER OF PEARL

THE PROCURATOR OF JUDÆA

. ÆLIUS LAMIA, born in Italy of illustrious parents, had not yet discarded the *toga prætexta* when he set out for the schools of Athens to study philosophy. Subsequently he took up his residence at Rome, and in his house on the Esquiline, amid a circle of youthful wastrels, abandoned himself to licentious courses. But being accused of engaging in criminal relations with Lepida, the wife of Sulpicius Quirinus, a man of consular rank, and being found guilty, he was exiled by Tiberius Cæsar. At that time he was just entering his twenty-fourth year. During the eighteen years that his exile lasted he traversed Syria, Palestine, Cappadocia, and Armenia, and made prolonged visits to Antioch, Cæsarea, and Jerusalem. When, after the death of Tiberius, Caius was raised to the purple, Lamia obtained permission to return to Rome. He even regained

a portion of his possessions. Adversity had taught him wisdom.

He avoided all intercourse with the wives and daughters of Roman citizens, made no efforts towards obtaining office, held aloof from public honours, and lived a secluded life in his house on the Esquiline. Occupying himself with the task of recording all the remarkable things he had seen during his distant travels, he turned, as he said, the vicissitudes of his years of expiation into a diversion for his hours of rest. In the midst of these calm employments, alternating with assiduous study of the works of Epicurus, he recognized with a mixture of surprise and vexation that age was stealing upon him. In his sixty-second year, being afflicted with an illness which proved in no slight degree troublesome, he decided to have recourse to the waters at Baiæ. The coast at that point, once frequented by the halcyon, was at this date the resort of the wealthy Roman, greedy of pleasure. For a week Lamia lived alone, without a friend in the brilliant crowd. Then one day, after dinner, an inclination to which he yielded urged him to ascend the incline, which, covered with vines that resembled bacchantes, looked out upon the waves.

Having reached the summit he seated himself by the side of a path beneath a terebinth, and let his glances wander over the lovely landscape. To his left, livid and bare, the Phlegræan plain stretched out towards the ruins of Cumæ. On his right, Cape Misenum plunged its abrupt spur beneath the Tyrrhenian sea. Beneath his feet luxurious Baiæ, following the graceful outline of the coast, displayed its gardens, its villas thronged with statues, its porticos, its marble terraces along the shores of the blue ocean where the dolphins sported. Before him, on the other side of the bay, on the Campanian coast, gilded by the already sinking sun, gleamed the temples which far away rose above the laurels of Posilippo, whilst on the extreme horizon Vesuvius looked forth smiling.

Lamia drew from a fold of his toga a scroll containing the *Treatise upon Nature*, extended himself upon the ground, and began to read. But the warning cries of a slave necessitated his rising to allow of the passage of a litter which was being carried along the narrow pathway through the vineyards. The litter being uncurtained, permitted Lamia to see stretched upon the cushions as it was borne nearer to him the figure of an elderly man of immense bulk, who, supporting his head on his hand, gazed out with a gloomy and disdainful expression. His nose, which was aquiline, and his chin, which was prominent, seemed desirous of meeting across his lips, and his jaws were powerful.

From the first moment Lamia was convinced that the face was familiar to him. He hesitated a moment before the name came to him. Then suddenly hastening towards the litter with a display of surprise and delight—

"Pontius Pilate!" he cried. "The gods be praised who have permitted me to see you once again!"

The old man gave a signal to the slaves to stop, and cast a keen glance upon the stranger who had addressed him.

"Pontius, my dear host," resumed the latter, "have twenty years so far whitened my hair and hollowed my cheeks that you no longer recognize your friend Ælius Lamia?"

At this name Pontius Pilate dismounted from the litter as actively as the weight of his years and the heaviness of his gait permitted him, and embraced Ælius Lamia again and again.

"Gods! what a treat it is to me to see you once more! But, alas, you call up memories of those long-vanished days when I was Procurator of Judæa in the province of Syria. Why, it must be thirty years ago that I first met you. It was at Cæsarea, whither you came to drag out your weary term of exile. I was fortunate enough to alleviate it a little, and out of friendship, Lamia, you followed me to that depressing place Jerusalem, where the Jews filled me with bitterness and dis-

gust. You remained for more than ten years my
guest and my companion, and in converse about
Rome and things Roman we both of us managed
to find consolation—you for your misfortunes, and
I for my burdens of State."

Lamia embraced him afresh.

"You forget two things, Pontius; you are over-
looking the facts that you used your influence on
my behalf with Herod Antipas, and that your
purse was freely open to me."

"Let us not talk of that," replied Pontius,
"since after your return to Rome you sent me by
one of your freedmen a sum of money which
repaid me with usury."

"Pontius, I could never consider myself out
of your debt by the mere payment of money. But
tell me, have the gods fulfilled your desires? Are
you in the enjoyment of all the happiness you
deserve? Tell me about your family, your fortunes, your health."

"I have withdrawn to Sicily, where I possess
estates, and where I cultivate wheat for the market.
My eldest daughter, my best-beloved Pontia, who
has been left a widow, lives with me, and directs
my household. The gods be praised, I have preserved my mental vigour; my memory is not in
the least degree enfeebled. But old age always
brings in its train a long procession of griefs and

infirmities. I am cruelly tormented with gout. And at this very moment you find me on my way to the Phlegræan plain in search of a remedy for my sufferings. From that burning soil, whence at night flames burst forth, proceed acrid exhalations of sulphur, which, so they say, ease the pains and restore suppleness to the stiffened joints. At least, the physicians assure me that it is so."

"May you find it so in your case, Pontius! But, despite the gout and its burning torments, you scarcely look as old as myself, although in reality you must be my senior by ten years. Unmistakably you have retained a greater degree of vigour than I ever possessed, and I am overjoyed to find you looking so hale. Why, dear friend, did you retire from the public service before the customary age? Why, on resigning your governorship in Judæa, did you withdraw to a voluntary exile on your Sicilian estates? Give me an account of your doings from the moment that I ceased to be a witness of them. You were preparing to suppress a Samaritan rising when I set out for Cappadocia, where I hoped to draw some profit from the breeding of horses and mules. I have not seen you since then. How did that expedition succeed? Pray tell me. Everything interests me that concerns you in any way."

Pontius Pilate sadly shook his head.

"My natural disposition," he said, "as well as a sense of duty, impelled me to fulfil my public responsibilities, not merely with diligence, but even with ardour. But I was pursued by unrelenting hatred. Intrigues and calumnies cut short my career in its prime, and the fruit it should have looked to bear has withered away. You ask me about the Samaritan insurrection. Let us sit down on this hillock. I shall be able to give you an answer in few words. Those occurrences are as vividly present to me as if they had happened yesterday.

"A man of the people, of persuasive speech —there are many such to be met with in Syria— induced the Samaritans to gather together in arms on Mount Gerizim (which in that country is looked upon as a holy place) under the promise that he would disclose to their sight the sacred vessels which in the ancient days of Evander and our father, Æneas, had been hidden away by an eponymous hero, or rather a tribal deity, named Moses. Upon this assurance the Samaritans rose in rebellion; but having been warned in time to forestall them, I dispatched detachments of infantry to occupy the mountain, and stationed cavalry to keep the approaches to it under observation.

"These measures of prudence were urgent. The rebels were already laying siege to the town

B

of Tyrathaba, situated at the foot of Mount Gerizim. I easily dispersed them, and stifled the as yet scarcely organized revolt. Then, in order to give a forcible example with as few victims as possible, I handed over to execution the leaders of the rebellion. But you are aware, Lamia, in what strait dependence I was kept by the proconsul Vitellius, who governed Syria not in, but against the interests of Rome, and looked upon the provinces of the empire as territories which could be farmed out to tetrarchs. The head-men among the Samaritans, in their resentment against me, came and fell at his feet lamenting. To listen to them, nothing had been further from their thoughts than to disobey Cæsar. It was I who had provoked the rising, and it was purely in order to withstand my violence that they had gathered together round Tyrathaba. Vitellius listened to their complaints, and handing over the affairs of Judæa to his friend Marcellus, commanded me to go and justify my proceedings before the Emperor himself. With a heart overflowing with grief and resentment I took ship. Just as I approached the shores of Italy, Tiberius, worn out with age and the cares of empire, died suddenly on the selfsame Cape Misenum, whose peak we see from this very spot magnified in the mists of evening. I demanded justice of Caius, his successor, whose perception was naturally acute, and who was acquainted with Syrian affairs. But marvel with me, Lamia, at the maliciousness of fortune, resolved on my discomfiture. Caius then had in his suite at Rome the Jew Agrippa, his companion, the friend of his childhood, whom he cherished as his own eyes. Now Agrippa favoured Vitellius, inasmuch as Vitellius was the enemy of Antipas, whom Agrippa pursued with his hatred. The Emperor adopted the prejudices of his beloved Asiatic, and refused even to listen to me. There was nothing for me to do but bow beneath the stroke of unmerited misfortune. With tears for my meat and gall for my portion, I withdrew to my estates in Sicily, where I should have died of grief if my sweet Pontia had not come to console her father. I have cultivated wheat, and succeeded in producing the fullest ears in the whole province. But now my life is ended ; the future will judge between Vitellius and me."

"Pontius," replied Lamia, "I am persuaded that you acted towards the Samaritans according to the rectitude of your character, and solely in the interests of Rome. But were you not perchance on that occasion a trifle too much influenced by that impetuous courage which has always swayed you ? You will remember that in Judæa it often happened that I who, younger than you, should naturally have been more impetuous than you, was obliged to urge you to clemency and suavity."

"Suavity towards the Jews!" cried Pontius Pilate. "Although you have lived amongst them, it seems clear that you ill understand those enemies of the human race. Haughty and at the same time base, combining an invincible obstinacy with a despicably mean spirit, they weary alike your love and your hatred. My character, Lamia, was formed upon the maxims of the divine Augustus. When I was appointed Procurator of Judæa, the world was already penetrated with the majestic ideal of the *pax romana*. No longer, as in the days of our internecine strife, were we witnesses to the sack of a province for the aggrandisement of a proconsul. I knew where my duty lay. I was careful that my actions should be governed by prudence and moderation. The gods are my witnesses that I was resolved upon mildness, and upon mildness only. Yet what did my benevolent intentions avail me? You were at my side, Lamia, when, at the outset of my career as ruler, the first rebellion came to a head. Is there any need for me to recall the details to you? The garrison had been transferred from Cæsarea to take up its winter quarters at Jerusalem. Upon the ensigns of the legionaries appeared the presentment of Cæsar. The inhabitants

of Jerusalem, who did not recognize the indwelling
divinity of the Emperor, were scandalized at this,
as though, when obedience is compulsory, it were
not less abject to obey a god than a man.   The
priests of their nation appeared before my tribunal
imploring me with supercilious humility to have
the ensigns removed from within the holy city.   Out
of reverence for the divine nature of Cæsar and the
majesty of the empire, I refused to comply.   Then
the rabble made common cause with the priests,
and all around the pretorium portentous cries of
supplication arose.   I ordered the soldiers to stack
their spears in front of the tower of Antonia, and
to proceed, armed only with sticks like lictors, to
disperse the insolent crowd.   But, heedless of blows,
the Jews continued their entreaties, and the more
obstinate amongst them threw themselves on the
ground and, exposing their throats to the rods,
deliberately courted death.   You were a witness of
my humiliation on that occasion, Lamia.   By the
order of Vitellius I was forced to send the insignia
back to Cæsarea.   That disgrace I had certainly
not merited.   Before the immortal gods I swear
that never once during my term of office did I
flout justice and the laws.   But I am grown old.
My enemies and detractors are dead.   I shall
die unavenged.   Who will now retrieve my
character?"

He moaned and lapsed into silence. Lamia replied—

"That man is prudent who neither hopes nor fears anything from the uncertain events of the future. Does it matter in the least what estimate men may form of us hereafter? We ourselves are after all our own witnesses, and our own judges. You must rely, Pontius Pilate, on the testimony you yourself bear to your own rectitude. Be content with your own personal respect and that of your friends. For the rest, we know that mildness by itself will not suffice for the work of government. There is but little room in the actions of public men for that indulgence of human frailty which the philosophers recommend."

"We'll say no more at present," said Pontius. "The sulphureous fumes which rise from the Phlegræan plain are more powerful when the ground which exhales them is still warm beneath the sun's rays. I must hasten on. Adieu! But now that I have rediscovered a friend, I should wish to take advantage of my good fortune. Do me the favour, Ælius Lamia, to give me your company at supper at my house to-morrow. My house stands on the seashore, at the extreme end of the town in the direction of Misenum. You will easily recognize it by the porch which bears a painting representing Orpheus surrounded by tigers and lions, whom he is charming with the strains from his lyre.

"Till to-morrow, Lamia," he repeated, as he climbed once more into his litter. "To-morrow we will talk about Judæa."

The following day at the supper hour Lamia presented himself at the house of Pontius Pilate. Two couches only were in readiness for occupants. Creditably but simply equipped, the table held a silver service in which were set out beccaficos in honey, thrushes, oysters from the Lucrine lake, and lampreys from Sicily. As they proceeded with their repast, Pontius and Lamia interchanged inquiries with one another about their ailments, the symptoms of which they described at considerable length, mutually emulous of communicating the various remedies which had been recommended to them. Then, congratulating themselves on being thrown together once more at Baiæ, they vied with one another in praise of the beauty of that enchanting coast and the mildness of the climate they enjoyed. Lamia was enthusiastic about the charms of the courtesans who frequented the seashore laden with golden ornaments and trailing draperies of barbaric broidery. But the aged Procurator deplored the ostentation with which by means of

trumpery jewels and filmy garments foreigners and
even enemies of the empire beguiled the Romans
of their gold. After a time they turned to the
subject of the great engineering feats that had been
accomplished in the country ; the prodigious bridge
constructed by Caius between Puteoli and Baiæ,
and the canals which Augustus excavated to convey
the waters of the ocean to Lake Avernus and the
Lucrine lake.

"I also," said Pontius, with a sigh, "I also
wished to set afoot public works of great utility.
When, for my sins, I was appointed Governor of
Judæa, I conceived the idea of furnishing Jerusalem with an abundant supply of pure water by
means of an aqueduct. The elevation of the
levels, the proportionate capacity of the various
parts, the gradient for the brazen reservoirs to which
the distribution pipes were to be fixed—I had gone
into every detail, and decided everything for myself
with the assistance of mechanical experts. I had
drawn up regulations for the superintendents so as
to prevent individuals from making unauthorized
depredations. The architects and the workmen
had their instructions. I gave orders for the com-
mencement of operations. But far from viewing
with satisfaction the construction of that conduit,
which was intended to carry to their town upon
its massive arches not only water but health, the

inhabitants of Jerusalem gave vent to lamentable outcries. They gathered tumultuously together, exclaiming against the sacrilege and impiousness, and, hurling themselves upon the workmen, scattered the very foundation stones. Can you picture to yourself, Lamia, a filthier set of barbarians? Nevertheless, Vitellius decided in their favour, and I received orders to put a stop to the work."

"It is a knotty point," said Lamia, "how far one is justified in devising things for the commonweal against the will of the populace."

Pontius Pilate continued as though he had not heard this interruption.

"Refuse an aqueduct! What madness! But whatever is of Roman origin is distasteful to the Jews. In their eyes we are an unclean race, and our very presence appears a profanation to them. You will remember that they would never venture to enter the pretorium for fear of defiling themselves, and that I was consequently obliged to discharge my magisterial functions in an open-air tribunal on that marble pavement your feet so often trod.

"They fear us and they despise us. Yet is not Rome the mother and warden of all those peoples who nestle smiling upon her venerable bosom? With her eagles in the van, peace and liberty have been carried to the very confines of the universe.

c

Those whom we have subdued we look on as our friends, and we leave those conquered races, nay, we secure to them the permanence of their customs and their laws. Did Syria, aforetime rent asunder by its rabble of petty kings, ever even begin to taste of peace and prosperity until it submitted to the armies of Pompey? And when Rome might have reaped a golden harvest as the price of her goodwill, did she lay hands on the hoards that swell the treasuries of barbaric temples? Did she despoil the shrine of Cybele at Pessinus, or the Morimene and Cilician sanctuaries of Jupiter, or the temple of the Jewish god at Jerusalem? Antioch, Palmyra, and Apamea, secure despite their wealth, and no longer in dread of the wandering Arab of the desert, have erected temples to the genius of Rome and the divine Cæsar. The Jews alone hate and withstand us. They withhold their tribute till it is wrested from them, and obstinately rebel against military service."

"The Jews," replied Lamia, "are profoundly attached to their ancient customs. They suspected you, unreasonably I admit, of a desire to abolish their laws and change their usages. Do not resent it, Pontius, if I say that you did not always act in such a way as to disperse their unfortunate illusion. It gratified you, despite your habitual self-restraint, to play upon their fears, and more than once have I seen you betray in their presence the contempt with which their beliefs and religious ceremonies inspired you. You irritated them particularly by giving instructions for the sacerdotal garments and ornaments of their high priest to be kept in ward by your legionaries in the Antonine tower. One must admit that though they have never risen like us to an appreciation of things divine, the Jews celebrate rites which their very antiquity renders venerable."

Pontius Pilate shrugged his shoulders.

"They have very little exact knowledge of the nature of the gods," he said. "They worship Jupiter, yet they abstain from naming him or erecting a statue of him. They do not even adore him under the semblance of a rude stone, as certain of the Asiatic peoples are wont to do. They know nothing of Apollo, of Neptune, of Mars, nor of Pluto, nor of any goddess. At the same time, I am convinced that in days gone by they worshipped Venus. For even to this day their women bring doves to the altar as victims ; and you know as well as I that the dealers who trade beneath the arcades of their temple supply those birds in couples for sacrifice. I have even been told that on one occasion some madman proceeded to overturn the stalls bearing these offerings, and their owners with them. The priests raised an outcry about it, and looked on it as a case of sacrilege. I am of opinion that their custom of sacrificing turtle-

doves was instituted in honour of Venus. Why
are you laughing, Lamia ?"

"I was laughing," said Lamia, "at an amusing
idea which, I hardly know how, just occurred to
me. I was thinking that perchance some day the
Jupiter of the Jews might come to Rome and vent
his fury upon you. Why should he not? Asia
and Africa have already enriched us with a considerable number of gods. We have seen temples
in honour of Isis and the dog-faced Anubis erected
in Rome. In the public squares, and even on the
race-courses, you may run across the Bona Dea of
the Syrians mounted on an ass. And did you
never hear how, in the reign of Tiberius, a young
patrician passed himself off as the horned Jupiter of
the Egyptians, Jupiter Ammon, and in this disguise procured the favours of an illustrious lady
who was too virtuous to deny anything to a god ?
Beware, Pontius, lest the invisible Jupiter of the
Jews disembark some day on the quay at Ostia ! "

At the idea of a god coming out of Judæa, a
fleeting smile played over the severe countenance
of the Procurator. Then he replied gravely—

"How would the Jews manage to impose their
sacred law on outside peoples when they are in a
perpetual state of tumult amongst themselves as to
the interpretation of that law ? You have seen
them yourself, Lamia, in the public squares, split

up into twenty rival parties, with staves in their hands, abusing each other and clutching one another by the beard. You have seen them on the steps of the temple, tearing their filthy garments as a symbol of lamentation, with some wretched creature in a frenzy of prophetic exaltation in their midst. They have never realized that it is possible to discuss peacefully and with an even mind those matters concerning the divine which yet are hidden from the profane and wrapped in uncertainty. For the nature of the immortal gods remains hidden from us, and we cannot arrive at a knowledge of it. Though I am of opinion, none the less, that it is a prudent thing to believe in the providence of the gods. But the Jews are devoid of philosophy, and cannot tolerate any diversity of opinions. On the contrary, they judge worthy of the extreme penalty all those who on divine subjects profess opinions opposed to their law. And as, since the genius of Rome has towered over them, capital sentences pronounced by their own tribunals can only be carried out with the sanction of the proconsul or the procurator, they harry the Roman magistrate at any hour to procure his signature to their baleful decrees, they besiege the pretorium with their cries of ' Death ! ' A hundred times, at least, have I known them, mustered, rich and poor together, all united under their priests, make a furious on-

slaught on my ivory chair, seizing me by the skirts
of my robe, by the thongs of my sandals, and all
to demand of me—nay, to exact from me—the death
sentence on some unfortunate whose guilt I failed
to perceive, and as to whom I could only pronounce
that he was as mad as his accusers. A hundred
times, do I say! Not a hundred, but every day
and all day. Yet it was my duty to execute their
law as if it were ours, since I was appointed by
Rome not for the destruction, but for the uphold-
ing of their customs, and over them I had the
power of the rod and the axe. At the outset of
my term of office I endeavoured to persuade them
to hear reason; I attempted to snatch their miserable victims from death. But this show of mildness only irritated them the more; they demanded
their prey, fighting around me like a horde of
vultures with wing and beak. Their priests reported to Cæsar that I was violating their law, and
their appeals, supported by Vitellius, drew down
upon me a severe reprimand. How many times
did I long, as the Greeks used to say, to dispatch
accusers and accused in one convoy to the crows!

"Do not imagine, Lamia, that I nourish the
rancour of the discomfited, the wrath of the super-
annuated, against a people which in my person has
prevailed against both Rome and tranquillity. But
I foresee the extremity to which sooner or later

they will reduce us. Since we cannot govern them, we shall be driven to destroy them. Never doubt it. Always in a state of insubordination, brewing rebellion in their inflammatory minds, they will one day burst forth upon us with a fury beside which the wrath of the Numidians and the mutterings of the Parthians are mere child's play. They are secretly nourishing preposterous hopes, and madly premeditating our ruin. How can it be otherwise, when, on the strength of an oracle, they are living in expectation of the coming of a prince of their own blood whose kingdom shall extend over the whole earth ? There are no half measures with such a people. They must be exterminated. Jerusalem must be laid waste to the very foundation. Perchance, old as I am, it may be granted me to behold the day when her walls shall fall and the flames shall envelop her houses, when her inhabitants shall pass under the edge of the sword, when salt shall be strown on the place where once the temple stood. And in that day I shall at length be justified."

Lamia exerted himself to lead the conversation back to a less acrimonious note.

"Pontius," he said, "it is not difficult for me to understand both your long-standing resentment and your sinister forebodings. Truly, what you have experienced of the character of the Jews is nothing

to their advantage. But I lived in Jerusalem as
an interested onlooker, and mingled freely with
the people, and I succeeded in detecting certain
obscure virtues in these rude folk which were altogether hidden from you. I have met Jews who
were all mildness, whose simple manners and faith-
fulness of heart recalled to me what our poets
have related concerning the Spartan lawgiver.
And you yourself, Pontius, have seen perish beneath the cudgels of your legionaries simple-
minded men who have died for a cause they
believed to be just without revealing their names.
Such men do not deserve our contempt. I am
saying this because it is desirable in all things to
preserve moderation and an even mind. But I
own that I never experienced any lively sympathy
for the Jews. The Jewesses, on the contrary, I
found extremely pleasing. I was young then, and
the Syrian women stirred all my senses to response.
Their ruddy lips, their liquid eyes that shone in
the shade, their sleepy gaze pierced me to the very
marrow. Painted and stained, smelling of nard
and myrrh, steeped in odours, their physical attrac-
tions are both rare and delightful."

Pontius listened impatiently to these praises.

"I was not the kind of man to fall into the
snares of the Jewish women," he said ; "and since
you have opened the subject yourself, Lamia, I

was never able to approve of your laxity. If I did
not express with sufficient emphasis formerly how
culpable I held you for having intrigued at Rome
with the wife of a man of consular rank, it was
because you were then enduring heavy penance for
your misdoings. Marriage from the patrician
point of view is a sacred tie; it is one of
the institutions which are the support of Rome.
As to foreign women and slaves, such relations as
one may enter into with them would be of little
account were it not that they habituate the body to
a humiliating effeminacy. Let me tell you that
you have been too liberal in your offerings to the
Venus of the Market-place; and what, above all, I
blame in you is that you have not married in
compliance with the law and given children to the
Republic, as every good citizen is bound to do."

But the man who had suffered exile under Tiberius
was no longer listening to the venerable magistrate.
Having tossed off his cup of Falernian, he was
smiling at some image visible to his eye alone.

After a moment's silence he resumed in a very
deep voice, which rose in pitch by little and little—
"With what languorous grace they dance, those
Syrian women! I knew a Jewess at Jerusalem who
used to dance in a poky little room, on a thread-
bare carpet, by the light of one smoky little lamp,
waving her arms as she clanged her cymbals. Her

loins arched, her head thrown back, and, as it were, dragged down by the weight of her heavy red hair, her eyes swimming with voluptuousness, eager, languishing, compliant, she would have made Cleopatra herself grow pale with envy. I was in love with her barbaric dances, her voice—a little raucous and yet so sweet—her atmosphere of incense, the semi-somnolescent state in which she seemed to live. I followed her everywhere. I mixed with the vile rabble of soldiers, conjurers, and extortioners with which she was surrounded. One day, however, she disappeared, and I saw her no more. Long did I seek her in disreputable alleys and taverns. It was more difficult to learn to do without her than to lose the taste for Greek wine. Some months after I lost sight of her, I learned by chance that she had attached herself to a small company of men and women who were followers of a young Galilean thaumaturgist. His name was Jesus; he came from Nazareth, and he was crucified for some crime, I don't quite know what. Pontius, do you remember anything about the man?"

Pontius Pilate contracted his brows, and his hand rose to his forehead in the attitude of one who probes the deeps of memory. Then after a silence of some seconds—

"Jesus?" he murmured, "Jesus—of Nazareth? I cannot call him to mind."

AMYCUS AND CELESTINE

TO GEORGES DE PORTO-RICHE

AMYCUS AND CELESTINE

PRONE upon the threshold of his rude cavern the hermit Celestine passed in prayer the eve of the Easter Festival, that unearthly night upon which the shuddering demons are hurled into the abyss. And whilst the shades still enveloped the earth, at the moment when the exterminating angel winged his flight across Egypt, Celestine shivered, for he was seized with anguish and unease. He heard from afar in the forest the cries of the wild cats and the shrill voices of the frogs. Immersed in the unholy darkness, he even doubted whether the glorious mystery could come to pass. But when he saw the first signals of the day, gladness entered into his heart together with the dawn ; he realized that Christ was risen from the dead, and cried—

"Jesus is arisen from the grave. Love has conquered death. Alleluia ! He is risen all glorious from the foot of the hill. Alleluia ! The whole creation is restored and made anew. Darkness and evil are put to flight. Light and pardon encompass the world. Alleluia ! "

A lark, awakened amidst the wheat, answered him with song.

" He is risen again. I have dreamed of nests and eggs—white eggs, flecked with brown. Alleluia ! He is risen again."

Then the hermit Celestine left his cavern to go to the neighbouring chapel and celebrate the holy Easter Feast.

As he passed through the forest he saw in the midst of a glade a splendid beech, whose bursting buds already gave passage to tiny leaves of a tender green. Garlands of ivy and fillets of wool were hung upon its branches, which spread out groundwards. Votive tablets fastened to its gnarled trunk spoke of youth and love, and here and there some Eros, fashioned in clay, shorn of garments and with outspread wings, balanced himself lightly upon a branch. At this sight the hermit Celestine knitted his whitened brows.

" It is the fairies' tree," he said, " and the country maidens, according to ancient custom, have laden it with offerings. My life is passed in struggling against these fairies, and no one could conceive the annoyance these tiny creatures cause me. They do not openly rebel against me. Each year at harvest time I exorcise the tree with the customary rites, and sing the Gospel of St. John to them.

"There is nothing better to be done. Holy water and the Gospel of St. John have power to put them to flight, and there is nothing more heard of the little damsels throughout the winter ; but in the spring back they come once more, and each year one must begin all over again.

"And they are subtle ; a single bush of hawthorn is large enough to shelter a whole swarm. And they cast their spells upon the young folks, both the youths and the maidens.

"As I have grown older my sight has become dim and now I can scarcely perceive their presence. They make a mock of me, sport under my nose and laugh in my beard. But when I was only twenty, I often saw them in the clearings dancing in circles beneath the light of the moon like garlands of flowers. Oh, Lord God, Thou who madest the heaven and the dew, praised be Thou in Thy works. But why didst Thou create unholy trees and fairy springs ? Why hast Thou planted beneath the hazel the screaming mandrake ? These things of nature seduce the young to sin, and are the cause of unnumbered labours to anchorites who, like myself, have undertaken the sanctification of Thy creatures. If only the Gospel of St. John still availed to put the demons to flight ! But it is no longer enough, and I am perplexed to know what to do."

And as the good hermit went sighing on his way, the tree—for it was a fairy tree—called to him with a fresh rustling.

"Celestine! Celestine! My buds are eggs— true Easter eggs. Alleluia! Alleluia!"

Celestine plunged into the wood without turning his head. He made his way with difficulty by a narrow path through the midst of thorns which tore his gown, when suddenly the road was barred to him by a young lad who came bounding out of a thicket. He was half-clothed in the skin of some beast, and was indeed rather a faun than a boy. His glance was penetrating, his nose flattened, his countenance laughing. His curly hair concealed the two little horns upon his stubborn forehead; his lips disclosed white pointed teeth; a fair forked beard descended from his chin. Upon his chest a golden down shone. He was agile and slender, and his cloven feet were hidden in the grass.

Celestine, who had made himself possessor of all the wisdom to be won by meditation, saw at once with whom he had to do, and raised his arm to make the sign of the cross. But the faun, seizing his hand, prevented him from completing the mighty spell.

"Good hermit," said he, "do not exorcise me.

For me, as for you, this day is a day of festival. You would be wanting in charity if you should plunge me in grief during the Easter Feast. If you are willing, we will stroll along together, and you will see that I am not malicious."

By good fortune Celestine was well versed in the sacred sciences. He recalled to himself in these circumstances that St. Jerome in the desert had had for fellow-travellers both satyrs and centaurs who had confessed the Truth.

He said to the faun—

"Faun raise a hymn to God. Declare: He is risen."

"He is indeed arisen," replied the faun. "And behold me all gladness thereupon."

Here the path widened, so that they walked side by side. The hermit became pensive, and reflected—

"He cannot be a demon since he has witnessed to the Truth. It is well that I refrained from grieving him. The example of the great St. Jerome has not been lost upon me."

Then, turning towards his goat-footed companion, he asked him—

"What is your name?"

"I am called Amycus," replied the faun. "I dwell in this wood, where I was born. I came to you, good father, because behind your long white

D

beard your countenance was kindly. It seems to
me that hermits must be fauns borne down by the
years. When I am grown old I shall be like unto
you."

"He is risen," said the hermit.

"He is indeed arisen," said Amycus.

And thus conversing they climbed the hill on
which arose a chapel consecrated to the true God.
It was small and of homely construction. Celestine
had built it with his own hands with the fragments
of a temple of Venus. Within, the table of the
Lord stood forth shapeless and uncovered.

"Let us fall down," said the hermit, "and sing
Alleluia, for He is arisen. And do you, mysterious
being, remain kneeling whilst I offer the holy
sacrifice."

But the faun drew near to the hermit, and stroked
his beard, and said—

"Venerable old man, you are wiser than I, and
you can discern that which is invisible. But the
woods and the springs are better known to me than
to you. I will bring to God leafage and blossoms.
I know the banks where the cress half opens its
lilac clusters, the meadows where the cowslip
blossoms in yellow bunches. I detect by its faint
odour the mistletoe upon the wild apple tree.
Already the blackthorn bushes are decked with a
snowy crown of flowers. Wait for me, good father."

With three goat-like leaps he was back in the woods, and when he returned Celestine fancied he beheld a walking hawthorn tree.   Amycus had disappeared beneath his odorous harvest. He hung garlands of flowers about the rustic altar; he sprinkled it with violets, and said solemnly—

"I dedicate these flowers to the God who gave them being."

And whilst Celestine celebrated the sacrifice of the mass, the goat-footed one bowed his horned head down to the very ground and worshipped the sun, and said—

"The earth is a vast egg which thou, O Sun, most holy Sun, dost render fruitful."

From that day forward Celestine and Amycus lived together in fellowship.   The hermit never succeeded, despite all his endeavours, in making the half-human creature understand the ineffable mysteries; but as through the exertions of Amycus the chapel of the true God was constantly hung with garlands, and more gaily decked than the fairies' tree, the holy priest said—

"The faun is himself a hymn to God."

And it was for this reason that he bestowed on him the rite of holy baptism.

Upon the hill where Celestine once raised the meagre chapel which Amycus garlanded with flowers from the hills, the woods, and the streams, there

stands at the present day a church the nave of
which goes back to the eleventh century, whilst the
porch dates from the period of Henry II, when it
was rebuilt in the style of the Renaissance.   It is a
place of pilgrimage, and the faithful assemble there
to hold in pious memory the saints Amycus and
Celestine.

THE LEGEND OF
SAINTS OLIVERIA AND LIBERETTA

TO MADEMOISELLE JEANNE POUQUET

THE LEGEND OF
SAINTS OLIVERIA AND LIBERETTA

CHAPTER I

How Messire St. Berthold, son of Theodulus, King of Scotland, came over to the Ardennes to preach to the inhabitants of the Pays Porcin.

HE forest of the Ardennes extended at that time as far as the waters of the Aisne, and covered the Pays Porcin, in which now rises the town of Rethel. Its ravines swarmed with innumerable wild boars, stags of immense height of a species now extinct thronged in the impenetrable thickets, and wolves of prodigious strength were encountered in winter on the skirts of the woods. The basilisk and the unicorn had their quarters in that forest, as well as a frightful dragon, which later on, by the grace of God, met with destruction at the prayers of a holy hermit. And because in those days the mysteries of nature were revealed to men, and for the glory of the Creator things

which were naturally invisible became visible, it
was common to meet in the clearings nymphs,
satyrs, centaurs, and aigypans.

Now it is in no respect doubtful that these male-
volent beings have indeed been seen just as they
have been described in the fables of the pagans.
But it must be remembered that they are devils, as
is apparent by their feet, which are cloven. Unhappily the fairies are not so easy to detect ; these
have all the appearance of damsels, and at times
the resemblance is so pronounced that one must
possess all the prudence of a hermit if one would
avoid being deceived. The fairies also are demons,
and there were in the forest of the Ardennes great
numbers of them. It was for this very reason that
that forest so abounded in mystery and horror.

The Romans in the time of Cæsar had consecrated it to Diana, and the inhabitants of the
Pays Porcin on the shores of the Aisne worshipped
an idol in the form of a woman. They made
offerings to her of cakes, milk, and honey, and
sang hymns in her honour.

Now Berthold, the son of Theodulus, King of
Scotland, having received holy baptism, lived in
the palace of his father, more after the fashion of
a hermit than of a prince. Close shut in his apartment, he spent the livelong day in reciting prayers
and meditating upon the Holy Scriptures, and the

desire kindled in him to imitate the labours of the apostles. Having learned through a miraculous source the abominations of the Pays Porcin, he straightway loathed and resolved to put an end to them.

He crossed the sea in a ship which had neither sail nor rudder, and which was drawn by a swan. Happily arrived in the Pays Porcin, he wandered through the villages, the walled towns, and the castles, announcing the glad tidings.

"The God whom I preach to you," he said, "is the only true God. He is one God in three Persons, and His Son was born of a Virgin."

But these rude men answered him—

"Youthful stranger, it is very simple on your part to imagine that there is but one God. For the gods are countless. They dwell in the woods, the mountains, and the streams. There are even gods so intimate that they do not disdain a place by the hearths of pious men. Others, again, take up their station in the stables and byres, and so the race of the gods fills the whole universe. But what you have to say about a Divine Virgin is not without warrant. We know of a Virgin with a threefold countenance to whom we sing canticles, and say, 'Hail most benign! Hail most terrible!' She is called Diana, and beneath her silvery tread under the pale beams of the moon the mountain thyme bursts into blossom. She has not disdained to receive upon her couch blossoming hyacinths, the offering of shepherds and huntsmen like ourselves. Nevertheless, she remains ever virgin."

Thus spake these ignorant men whilst they drove the apostle to the confines of the village, and pursued him with mocking words.

CHAPTER II

*Of the meeting between Messire St. Berthold and the
two sisters Oliveria and Liberetta.*

OW one day as he pursued his
journey, overcome with weariness
and grief, he fell in with two young
girls, who were setting forth from
their castle for a jaunt in the woods.
He made several steps towards them, and then
stood off at a distance for fear of alarming them,
and said—

"Give ear, young virgins. I am Berthold, son
of Theodulus, King of Scotland. But I have disdained perishable crowns that I might be worthy
at last to receive at the hand of the angels the
Crown that fadeth not away. And I journeyed
hither in a ship, drawn by a swan, to bring you
the glad tidings."

"Sir Berthold," replied the elder, "my name
is Oliveria, and that of my sister is Liberetta.
Our father, Thierry, who is also called Porphyrodimus, is the wealthiest lord in the country.
Willingly will we listen to your good tidings.

But you appear overcome with fatigue. I counsel you to go and await us in the hall of our father, who is at this moment drinking the good ale with his friends. When he learns that you are a Scottish prince, he will without question assign you a place at his table. Farewell, till we meet again, Sir Berthold. We are going, my sister and I, to gather flowers as an offering to Diana."

But the apostle Berthold replied—

"It is not for me to go and seat myself at a pagan's table. This Diana whom you imagine to be a heavenly virgin is in very truth a demon out of hell. The true God is one God in three Persons, and Jesus Christ His Son became Man and died upon the cross for the salvation of all men. And verily I tell you, Oliveria and Liberetta, a drop of His blood flowed on behalf of each one of you."

Then he discoursed to them with so much ardour of the holy mysteries, that the hearts of the two sisters were moved thereby. The elder sister took up the discourse anew.

"Sir Berthold," she said, "you disclose unheard-of mysteries. But it is not always an easy matter to distinguish truth from error. It would be painful to us to abandon our devotion to Diana. Nevertheless, let but a sign of the truth of your words appear to us, and we will believe in Jesus crucified."

But the younger sister said to the apostle—

"My sister Oliveria has asked for a sign because she is of a prudent nature and full of wisdom. But if your God is the true God, Sir Berthold, would that I might know and love Him without being impelled by a sign."

The man of God understood by these words that Liberetta was born to become a great saint. And on this account he replied—

"Sister Liberetta and Sister Oliveria, I have resolved to retire into that forest, there to lead the eremitical life which is both desirable and rare. I shall dwell in a hut of interlaced boughs, and support life upon roots. I shall pray unceasingly to God to change the hearts of the men of this country, and I shall bestow my benediction on the springs, so that the fairy folk may cease to come thither for the beguiling of sinners. Nevertheless, my sister Oliveria shall receive the sign for which she has asked. And a messenger sent by the Lord himself shall guide you both to my hermitage in order that I may instruct you in the faith of Jesus Christ."

Having spoken after this fashion, St. Berthold gave his blessing to the two sisters with the imposition of hands. After which he fared forth into the forest, from which he never afterwards emerged.

CHAPTER III

How the unicorn came to the hall of Thierry, otherwise called Porphyrodimus, and conducted the two sisters Oliveria and Liberetta to the retreat of Messire St. Berthold, and of divers marvels that ensued.

OW one day, being alone in the kitchen, Oliveria was spinning wool beneath the chimney canopy when she saw approach her a beast of a perfect whiteness which had the body of a goat and the head of a horse, and which bore on its forehead a shining spear. Oliveria immediately recognized what animal it was, and as she had maintained her innocence she was not in the least afraid, being aware that the unicorn never does any harm to discreet maidens. And indeed the unicorn did but place his head gently upon Oliveria's knees. Then turning again towards the door, by the direction of its eyes it invited the young girl to follow it without.

Oliveria immediately called her sister, but when Liberetta entered the room the unicorn had disappeared; and so it came about that Liberetta, in accordance with her desire, acknowledged the true God without having been constrained by a sign.

The two sisters set forth in the direction of the forest, and the unicorn, who had once more become visible, walked ahead of them. They pursued throughout their journey the trail of the wild beasts. And it came to pass that when they had reached the depths of the wood, they saw the unicorn take to the water and swim across a torrent. Now when they came to the water's edge they were aware that it was both wide and deep. They leaned over it to see if perchance there might be any stepping-stones by means of which they could cross, but none such could they discover. Now whilst they were leaning upon a willow and gazing upon the foaming waters, the tree bent down suddenly and bore them without effort to the opposite shore.

Thus, then, they arrived at the hermitage, where St. Berthold imparted unto them the words of life. Upon their return, the willow uprearing itself again bore them back to the other side.

Each day they betook themselves to the dwelling of the holy man, and when they returned to their own home they found that all the thread on their distaffs had been spun by invisible hands. For these reasons, then, having received baptism, they believed in Jesus Christ.

For more than a year they received instruction
from St. Berthold, when Thierry their father, who
was also called Porphyrodimus, was seized with
a cruel malady. Being aware that the end of their
father was drawing nigh, his daughters instructed
him in the Christian faith. He acknowledged the
truth. And so it came about that his death was
most meritorious. He was ensepulchred near to
his mortal home in a place known as the Giant's
Mountain, and in after days his tomb was venerated
throughout the Pays Porcin.

Meanwhile the two sisters repaired daily to the
dwelling of the holy hermit Berthold, and they
gathered from his lips the words of life. But on
a certain day when the rivers were greatly swollen
by the melted snows, Oliveria, as she went through
the vineyards, took a prop that she might with
greater security cross the torrent whose much
widened stream sped along riotously.

Liberetta, disdaining all human aid, declined to
follow her example. She was the first to reach
the torrent, her hands armed solely with the sign
of the cross. And the willow bent down in its
customary way. Then it rose erect once more,
and when Oliveria in her turn desired to pass over
it remained motionless. And the current broke
her prop as if it had been a wisp of straw and
carried it away. And Oliveria remained still on

the hither side. But since she was discreet she
recognized that she was justly punished for having
doubted the heavenly powers, and for not having
committed herself to the grace of God after the
manner of her sister Liberetta. Thereafter she
had no other thought but to win pardon for herself
by works of penitence and self-denial. So being
resolved, after the example of St. Berthold, to lead
the eremitical life which is both desirable and rare,
she remained in the forest on this side of the
torrent, and built herself a hut of boughs interlaced at a spot where a spring gushed forth, which
has since received the name of St. Olive's well.

E

CHAPTER IV

How Messire St. Berthold, and Mesdames Saints Liberetta and Oliveria came to their blissful consummation.

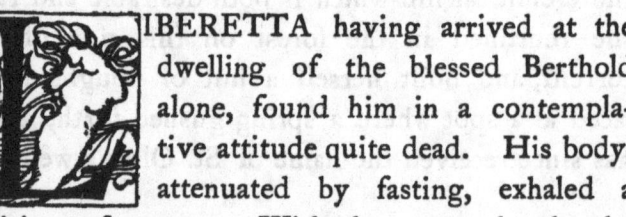

IBERETTA having arrived at the dwelling of the blessed Berthold alone, found him in a contemplative attitude quite dead. His body, attenuated by fasting, exhaled a delicious fragrance. With her own hands she buried him. From this day forward the virgin Liberetta, having taken leave of the world, led the eremitical life on the other side of the torrent, in a hut by the edge of a spring, which has since been known as the well of St. Liberetta, or Liberia, whose miraculous waters cure fevers as well as divers maladies with which cattle are afflicted.

The two sisters never saw one another again in this world. But, by the intercession of the blessed Berthold, God sent into the Ardennes from the country of the Lombards the deacon Vulfaï, or Valfroy, who overturned the idol of Diana and converted the inhabitants of the Pays Porcin to

the Christian faith.   Thereupon Oliveria and
Liberetta were overwhelmed with joy.

But a little time after this the Lord called to
Himself his servant Liberetta, and sent the unicorn
to dig a grave and bury the body of the saint.
Oliveria was aware, through a revelation, of the
blissful death of her sister, Liberetta, and a voice
said to her—

" Because you asked for a sign before you would
believe, and took a prop to lean upon, the hour of
your blissful death will be delayed and the day of
your consummation postponed."

And Oliveria replied to the voice—

" May the will of the Lord be done on earth as
it is in heaven."

She lived ten years longer in expectation of
eternal beatitude, which commenced for her in the
month of October, in the year of Our Lord 364.

ST. EUPHROSINE

TO GASTON-ARMAN DE CAILLAVET

ST. EUPHROSINE

The acts of St. Euphrosine of Alexandria, in religion Brother Smaragdus, as they were set forth in the Laura on Mount Athos by George the Deacon.

UPHROSINE was the only daughter of a rich citizen of Alexandria, named Romulus, who was careful to have her instructed in music, dancing, and arithmetic in such fashion that at the close of her childhood she displayed a subtle and unusually adorned intelligence. She had not yet completed her eleventh year when the magistrates of Alexandria caused to be announced in the streets that a golden cup would be awarded as a prize to whomsoever should produce an exact reply to the three following questions.

First Question : I am the dusky child of a luminous sire ; a wingless bird, yet I rise to the clouds. With no spark of malice, I yet draw tears from the eyes I encounter. Scarcely am I born when I vanish into air. Tell me, friend, what is my name ?

Second Question : I beget my mother, yet am

by her brought forth, and sometimes I am longer and sometimes shorter. Tell me, friend, what is my name?

Third Question : Antipater possesses as much as Nicomedes and a third of the share of Themistius. Nicomedes possesses as much as Themistius and a third of what Antipater owns. Themistius possesses ten minas and a third of what Nicomedes owns. What is the sum which belongs to each?

Now, on the day set apart for the gathering, a number of young men presented themselves before the judges in the hope of winning the golden cup, but not one of them gave correct replies. The president was about to bring the sitting to an end when the youthful Euphrosine, in her turn drawing near to the tribunal, asked to be heard. Every one admired the modesty of her bearing and the winsome shamefacedness which lent a blush to her cheeks.

"Most illustrious judges," she said, lowering her eyes, "after having given the glory to our Lord Jesus Christ, the beginning and the end of all wisdom, I will endeavour to reply to the questions which your worships have propounded, and I will begin with the first. The dusky child is smoke, which is born of fire, rises in the air, and by its pungency draws tears from our eyes. So much for the first question.

"Now to reply to the second. That which begets its mother and is by her brought forth is nothing other than the day, which is sometimes long and sometimes short, according to the season. So much for the second question.

"And now to answer the third. Antipater possesses forty-five minas, Nicomedes has but thirty-seven and a half, whilst Themistius has twenty-two and a half. That is my third answer."

The judges, marvelling at the correctness of these replies, awarded the prize to the youthful Euphrosine. Thereupon the most venerable among them, having risen, presented her with the golden cup, and encircled her forehead with a garland of papyrus by way of honouring the keen intelligence she had displayed. Then the virgin was conducted home to her father's house to the sound of flutes amidst a great concourse of people.

But as she was a Christian and pious in no ordinary degree, far from being puffed up with these honours, she recognized their emptiness, and resolved that in the future she would apply the keenness of her intelligence to the solution of problems more worthy of attention—as, for example, the computation of the sum of the numbers represented by the letters of the name of Jesus, and the consideration of the wonderful properties of these numbers.

Meanwhile she grew in wisdom and in beauty, and was sought in marriage by very many young men. Amongst these was the Count Longinus, who possessed great wealth. Romulus received this suitor favourably, hoping that an alliance with this powerful man might assist him in the re-habilitation of his own affairs, which had got into disorder through his vast expenditure upon his palace, his plate, and his gardens. Romulus, who was one of the most lavish amongst the inhabi-tants of Alexandria, had above all squandered considerable sums in gathering together in his mansion, beneath a vast cupola, the most wonderful examples of mechanism, such as a globe as brilliant as a sapphire, bearing on it the heavenly constella-tions set out with exactitude in precious stones. There were also to be seen in this chamber a fountain, constructed by Hero, which distributed perfumed waters, and two mirrors so cunningly contrived that they converted the gazer, the one into a person of extreme height and slenderness, and the other into a person equally short and stout. But the most marvellous sight in this mansion was a hawthorn bush all covered with birds, which by ingenious mechanism both sang and fluttered their wings as if they had been alive. Romulus had expended the remains of his wealth in the acquisition of these mechanical toys, which fascinated him. This, then, was the reason for his favourable reception of the Count Longinus, the possessor of great wealth. He urged forward by all means in his power the consummation of a marriage from which he anticipated both happiness for his daughter and relief from anxiety in his old age. But each time that he recounted to Euphrosine the claims of Count Longinus, she turned her glance aside without making any reply. One day he said to her—

"Will you not admit, my daughter, that he is the handsomest, the wealthiest, and the noblest citizen in all Alexandria?"

Euphrosine replied discreetly—

"Willingly do I admit it, dear father. Indeed, I am convinced that Count Longinus surpasses all the citizens of this town in noble birth, worldly possessions, and personal beauty. Consequently, if I refuse to accept him as a husband there is little likelihood that any other will succeed where he has failed, and induce me to change my resolution, which is to consecrate my virginity to Jesus Christ."

When he heard of this determination Romulus fell into a violent passion, and swore that he knew well enough how to force Euphrosine to espouse Count Longinus; and without breaking forth into idle threats, he added that this marriage was resolved upon in his mind, and that it would be carried through without delay, whilst if his paternal authority did not suffice he would add to it that of the Emperor, who being divine, would not allow a daughter to disobey her father in a matter which was of so much public and State importance as the marriage of a woman of patrician rank.

Euphrosine was aware that her father had great influence with the Emperor, who at that time lived at Constantinople. She perceived that in this perilous situation she had no hope of assistance except from Count Longinus himself. On this account she entreated him to come to her in the basilica for a private interview.

Impelled by hope as well as curiosity, Count Longinus betook himself to the basilica all bedecked with gold and precious stones. The maiden did not make him wait. But when he saw her appear with dishevelled hair, wrapped in a black veil like a suppliant, he drew an evil augury from the sight, and his heart was disturbed.

Euphrosine was the first to speak.

"Most illustrious Longinus," she said to him, "if you love me as much as you declare, you will fear to do aught displeasing to me ; and, indeed, it would be giving me a mortal blow were you to lead me away to your house to have your pleasure of this body, which, with my soul, I have dedicated to

Our Lord Jesus Christ, the beginning and the end of all love."

But Count Longinus answered her—

"Most illustrious Euphrosine, love is stronger even than our wills; that is why it behoves us to bow before him as before a jealous master. I shall act towards you after the fashion he ordains, which is to take you for my wife."

"Is it becoming that a man—an illustrious man, too—should rob the Lord of His betrothed?"

"As to that, I shall take counsel from the bishops rather than from you."

These plans threw the young girl into the most lively consternation. She realized that she had no compassion to expect from this man of violence, governed altogether by his senses, and that the bishops could not enforce recognition of secret vows made by her to God in solitude. And in the excess of her uneasiness she had recourse to an artifice so singular that it is more to be marvelled at than held up as an example.

Her resolution being taken, she feigned to yield to the wishes of her father and the entreaties of her lover. She even suffered them to fix a day for the ceremony of betrothal. Count Longinus had already caused the jewels and ornaments destined for his bride to be placed in the marriage coffers; he had ordered for her twelve gowns, upon which were embroidered scenes from the Old and the New Testament, the legends of the Greeks, the history of animals, as well as the divine presentments of the Emperor and Empress, with their retinue of lords and ladies. One of these coffers, moreover, contained books upon theology and arithmetic written in letters of gold upon sheets of parchment, purple tinctured, and preserved between plates of ivory and gold.

Euphrosine, however, remained the day long shut up alone in her chamber, and the reason she gave for her withdrawal was that it behoved her to make ready her wedding garments.

"It would be most unfitting," she said, "if certain portions of my vesture should be shaped and sewn by any other hands than mine."

And in very truth she wielded her needle from morning till night. But that which she made ready secretly in this fashion was neither the symbolical veil of the virgin nor the white robe of the betrothed. What she prepared was the rough hood, short tunic, and loose breeches which the young artisans in towns are accustomed to wear while engaged in their labours. And whilst she fulfilled this undertaking she constantly invoked Jesus Christ, the beginning and the end of all the achievements of the upright. For this cause, then, she happily completed her clandestine task on the eighth day before that which had been fixed for the solemnization of the marriage. She remained all that day in prayer ; then, after having presented herself, according to her custom, to receive her father's kiss, she returned to her chamber and cut off her hair, which fell to her feet like skeins of gold, donned her short tunic, fastened the breeches about her waist with woollen straps, drew the hood down over her eyes, and, night having fallen, noiselessly left the house whilst all, masters and servants alike, were sleeping. Only the dog was still awake, but as he knew her he followed her for a short time in silence, and then returned to his kennel.

With rapid steps she made her way through the deserted city, where the only sounds audible were the occasional cries of drunken sailors and the heavy tread of the watchmen on duty in pursuit of robbers. And since God was with her she suffered no insult from man. Then, having passed through one of the gates of Alexandria, she set out towards the desert, following the course of the canals covered with papyrus and blue lotus. At the break of day she passed through a wretched village of working people. An old man was singing in front of his door whilst he polished a coffin made of sycamore wood. When she came abreast of him, he raised his hairy and featureless face, and cried out—

"By Jupiter! here comes the infant Eros, carrying a little pot of ointment to his mother! How delicate and pretty he is. In truth, he sparkles with attractiveness. They are liars who say that the gods have departed. For this youth is a veritable little god."

Then the prudent Euphrosine, informed by this speech that the old man was a pagan, had pity upon his ignorance, and prayed to God for his salvation. That prayer was granted. The old man, who was a coffin-maker, bearing the name of Porou, was in course of time converted, and took the name of Philotheos.

Now, after a journey of a whole day, Euphrosine arrived at a monastery where, under the governance of the abbot Onophrius, six hundred monks observed the admirable rule of St. Pacomius. She asked to be led before Onophrius, and said to him—

"My father, I am called Smaragdus, and I am an orphan. I beg you to receive me into your holy habitation, to the end that I may there enjoy the delights of fasting and repentance."

The abbot Onophrius, who had then attained the age of one hundred and six years, replied—

"Smaragdus, my child, beautiful are your feet,

for they have guided you to this dwelling; beautiful are your hands, for they have knocked at this door. You hunger and thirst after fasting and abstinence. Come, and you shall be satisfied. Happy the child who flies from the world whilst yet he wears his robe of innocence. The souls of men are exposed to deadly perils in the towns, and particularly in Alexandria, on account of the women who flock there in great numbers. Woman is to man so great a danger that even at my age the thought alone sends a shudder through all my frame. If one with sufficient effrontery should presume to enter into this holy house, my arm would suddenly recover its strength to hale her hence with heavy blows from this pastoral cross. It is our duty, my son, to worship God in all His works; but it is a profound mystery of His providence that He should have created woman. Stay with us, Smaragdus, my child; for it is certainly God who has led you hither."

After having been received in this fashion into the family of the holy man Onophrius, Euphrosine donned the monastic habit.

In her cell she praised the Lord, and rejoiced in her pious fraud upon this consideration, that her father and her lover would not fail to make search for her in all the convents for women in order to apprehend her by order of the Emperor, but that

F

they would never succeed in finding her in this refuge where Jesus Christ Himself had lovingly hidden her.

For three years she led the most edifying life in her cell, and the virtues of the youthful Smaragdus perfumed the monastery. For this cause the abbot Onophrius entrusted her with the duties of guest-master or porter, counting upon the prudence of the young monk as to the reception of strangers, and above all the exclusion of any women who might attempt to enter the monastery. For, said the holy man, woman is impure, and the mere mark of her footsteps is an infectious pollution.

Now Smaragdus had been guest-master for five years, when a stranger knocked at the door of the monastery. It was a man who was still young; his habiliments were magnificent, and he retained a remnant of pride; but he was pale and emaciated, and his eyes were inflamed with a restless melancholy.

"Brother guest-master," said this man, "conduct me into the presence of the holy abbot Onophrius, that he may assoil me, for I am a prey to a mortal ill."

Smaragdus, having begged the stranger to seat himself upon a stool, informed him that Onophrius, having reached his hundred and fourteenth year, had, in view of his approaching end, gone to visit the caves of the Holy Anchorites, Amon and Orcisus.

At this news the visitor sank down upon the stool and hid his head in his hands.

"I can no longer hope for healing, then," he murmured.

And raising his head again, he added—

"It is the love of a woman that has reduced me to this miserable state."

Not till then did Euphrosine recognize Count Longinus. She feared that he likewise might recognize her. But she soon reassured herself, and was seized with pity to see him looking so cast down and discomfited.

After a long silence, Count Longinus exclaimed—

"I would fain become a monk to escape from my despair."

Then he told the story of his love, and how his betrothed, Euphrosine, had suddenly disappeared; how for eight years he had sought her and failed to find her, and how he was consumed and wasted with love and grief.

She answered him with a gentleness that was heavenly.

"My lord, this Euphrosine, whose love you so bitterly deplore, was not worthy of so much love. Her beauty was not so precious, except in the ideal you yourself have formed of it; in truth, it is vile and contemptible. It was perishable, and what remains of it is not worth a regret. You believe yourself unable to live without Euphrosine, and yet, if you should happen to meet her, you might even fail to recognize her."

Count Longinus answered not a word, but this speech, or possibly the voice in which it was pronounced, made a happy impression on his soul. He departed in a more tranquil mood, and promised to return.

And indeed he did return, and being desirous of embracing the monastic life, he asked the holy abbot Onophrius for a cell, and made a gift to the monastery of all his possessions, which were immense. This was a source of great satisfaction to Euphrosine. But some time after this her heart was overwhelmed with a still greater joy.

It was in this way. A beggar, bending beneath the weight of his satchel and having only sordid rags to cover his nakedness, came to ask a morsel of bread from the charitable monks. In him Euphrosine recognized Romulus, her father; but pretending not to know who he was, she made him sit down, washed his feet, and set food before him.

"Child of God," said the beggar, "I was not always a penniless wanderer such as now you see me. Once I possessed great wealth and a very beautiful daughter, who was also very prudent and very learned. She unravelled the enigmas propounded in the public competitions, and on one occasion even received from the magistrates the papyrus crown. I lost her—I lost all my possessions. I am consumed with regret for my daughter and my wealth. I had above all things a bush full of birds which, by a marvellous contrivance, sang as though naturally. And now I have not even a mantle to cover me. Nevertheless, I should be comforted if before I die I might see once again my well-beloved daughter."

As he concluded these words Euphrosine threw herself at his feet, and said through her tears—

"My father, I am Euphrosine, your daughter, who one night fled from your house. And the dog did not bark. Your pardon, my father. For I have not accomplished these things except by the permission of our Lord Jesus Christ."

And after she had recounted to the old man the manner of her flight, disguised as a workman, to that very house where she had since passed eight peaceful years in hiding, she showed him a mark she had upon her neck. And by this sign Romulus recognized his daughter. He embraced her tenderly and bathed her in his tears, marvelling at the mysterious workings of the Lord.

And for this reason he resolved to become a

monk and to take up his abode in the monastery of
the holy abbot Onophrius. With his own hands
he built himself a cell of reeds next to that of
Count Longinus. They chanted the psalms and
cultivated the ground. During the hours of rest
they conversed upon the vanity of earthly affections and the riches of this world. But Romulus
never disclosed anything to anybody concerning
his wonderful recognition of his daughter Euphrosine, thinking it much for the best that Count
Longinus and the abbot Onophrius should learn the
details of her adventures in Paradise, when they
would have attained a full understanding of the
ways of God. Longinus never knew that his
betrothed was close beside him. All three lived for
several years longer in the practice of all the virtues,
and by the special favour of Providence they all
three fell asleep in the Lord almost at the same
time. Count Longinus passed away first. Romulus
died two months later, and St. Euphrosine, after
she had closed his eyes, was during the same week
called to heaven by Jesus Christ with the words :
"Come, my dove." St. Onophrius followed them
to the tomb, to which he descended full of
merits in the hundred and thirty-second year
of his age, on the holy day of Easter, in the
year 395 after the incarnation of the Son of God.
May the Archangel St. Michael make intercession

for us! Here end the acts of St. Euphrosine.
Amen.

Such is the narrative of George the Deacon,
written in the Laura on Mount Athos at a period
which may vary from the seventh to the fourteenth
century of the Christian era. As to this I waver,
since it is a matter of great uncertainty. This
narrative is now for the first time published; I have
the best of reasons for being sure on this point.
I should be glad to have equally good reasons for
thinking that it deserved to be put forth. I have
translated with a fidelity which has doubtless been
only too perceptible since it has infected my own
style with a Byzantine stiffness the inconvenience
of which seems to myself almost intolerable.
George the Deacon told his tale with less graceful-
ness than Herodotus, or Plutarch even. So that
one may perceive by his example that periods of
decadence are sometimes less impregnated with
charm and daintiness than is the common opinion
nowadays. This demonstration is perhaps the
principal merit my work can claim. That work will
be criticized vigorously, and no doubt questions
may be put to me to which I may find it difficult to
reply. The text which I have followed is not in
the hand of George the Deacon. I do not know if
it is complete. I foresee that lacunæ and inter-
pellations will be pointed out. Monsieur Schlum-

berger will hold in suspicion various formularies
employed in the course of the narrative, and Monsieur Alfred Rambaud will question the episode of
the old man Porou. I reply beforehand that, having
but a single text, I could do no other than follow
it. It is in very bad condition and hardly legible.
But one is bound to declare that all the masterpieces of classical antiquity in which we take such
delight have come down to us in the same condition. I have excellent reasons for believing that in
transcribing the text of my Deacon I have made
tremendous blunders, and that my translation teems
with misconceptions. Possibly even it is nothing
but a misconception from beginning to end. If
this should not appear so patently as one might
fear, it is because invariably the most unintelligible
text has some sort of meaning to him who trans-
lates it. Were this not the case, erudition would
cease to have any reason for continued existence.
I have compared the narrative of George the Deacon
with the passages in Rufinus and St. Jerome relating to St. Euphrosine. I am bound to say that it
does not altogether agree with them. It is doubtless for this reason that my publisher has inserted
this learned work in a light collection of tales.

SCHOLASTICA

TO MAURICE SPRONCK

SCHOLASTICA

T the time of which we speak, which was the fourth century of the Christian era, the youthful Injuriosus, only son of a senator of Auvergne (so the municipal officers were called), sought in marriage a young girl named Scholastica, who, like himself, was the only child of a senator. His suit was favourably received. And the marriage ceremony having been celebrated, he conducted her to his house, and led her into the bridal chamber. Whereupon, with a mournful countenance, she turned herself to the wall and wept bitterly.

"What is the cause of your distress? Tell me, I beg of you."

Then, as she maintained silence, he added—

"I entreat you by our Lord Jesus Christ, the Son of God, to show me plainly the reason for your lamentations."

Then she turned towards him and said—

"If I were to weep every day of life that remains to me, I should not shed tears enough to express the profound grief with which my heart is filled. This feeble body I had determined to preserve in all purity, and to present my virginity as an offering to Jesus Christ. Alas, and woe is me! that I am in such a fashion forsaken as to be unable to fulfil what I had resolved upon! Oh, day which never should have dawned upon me! Behold me severed from the heavenly spouse who had promised me paradise for a marriage portion, and become the bride of a mortal man, whilst that head which should have been crowned with the roses of immortality, is decked, or rather disfigured, with roses which already begin to wither. Alas! that body which upon the margin of the fourfold stream of the Lamb should have been endued with the garment of purity, bears instead the vile burden of the nuptial veil. Ah! why was not the first day of my life even also the last? Happy had I been had I entered the gates of death ere a single drop of milk had passed my lips! Oh, that the kisses of my gentle nurses had been bestowed upon my bier! When you hold out your hands towards me, I recall the hands which for the salvation of the world were pierced with nails."

And as she finished these words she wept bitterly.

The young man answered her persuasively—

"Scholastica, our parents are of the rich and noble amongst the dwellers in Auvergne, nor have yours more than a single daughter nor mine than an only son. They wished for our union as a means of continuing their families, lest after their death a stranger should enter into possession of their belongings."

But Scholastica replied—

"This world is nothing, and riches are nothing, and this life itself is nothing. Is that life which is nothing but a waiting upon death? They alone live who, in unending blessedness, bathe in the Light, and know the joy of angels in the possession of God."

At this moment Injuriosus, touched by grace, exclaimed—

"Ah, sweet and simple words, the light of life eternal glances upon my eyes! Scholastica, if you wish to hold fast to that you have resolved, I also at your side will lead a virgin life."

More than half reassured, and already smiling through her tears, she said—

"Injuriosus, for a man to grant to a woman a boon such as this is a difficult matter. But if you should procure that we keep ourselves unspotted from the world, a part of the marriage portion which my spouse and Lord Jesus Christ has promised to me will I give unto you."

Then, fortified by the sign of the cross, he said—

"I shall do that which you desire."

And clasping one another's hands, they fell asleep.

And from that time forward, sharing the same nuptial couch, they passed their days in un-exampled chastity. After ten years of trial Scholastica died.

According to the customs of the day, her body was borne into the basilica, in gala dress, and with uncovered face, to the chant of psalms, and followed by the whole populace.

Kneeling down beside her, in a loud voice Injuriosus uttered these words—

"I give Thee hearty thanks, Lord Jesus, that Thou hast bestowed upon me strength to preserve Thy treasure uninjured."

Upon these words, she that was dead rose up upon her funeral couch and smiled, and murmured softly—

"My friend, why do you declare that which no man has asked of you?"

Whereupon she resumed her everlasting rest.

Injuriosus soon followed her to the tomb. They buried him not far from her in the basilica of Saint Allire. The first night after he was laid there a miraculous rose tree sprang from the grave of the virgin bride and enwrapped both tombs in its flower-besprent embraces. So that on the morrow the folk beheld them bound fast one to the other by chains of roses. Recognizing by this sign the sanctity of the blessed Injuriosus and the blessed Scholastica, the priests of Auvergne held up these shrines to the veneration of the faithful. But in this province, which had been evangelized by Saints Allire and Nepotian, pagans still dwelt. One of these, by name Sylvanus, still held sacred the springs dedicated to the nymphs, hung votive pictures upon the branches of an ancient oak, and cherished by his fireside little images in clay representing the sun and the goddesses of fruitfulness. Half hidden amid the foliage, the garden god watched over his orchard. Sylvanus passed his declining years in the writing of verse. He composed eclogues and elegies in a style a little stiff perhaps, but not wanting in skill, and into these poems, whenever he could manage to do so, he introduced verses from the bards of old. With the general populace he too visited the spot where the Christian spouses were laid, and the good man marvelled at the rose tree which decked the two tombs. And as, after his fashion, he was pious, he recognized therein a heavenly sign. But he attributed the prodigy to his own gods, and doubted nothing that the rose tree flourished by the will of Eros.

Said he : " Now that she is nothing but a vain shadow, the tristful Scholastica regrets the hours

when love was timely and the pleasures she re-
nounced. These roses, which come forth from
her body and express her thoughts, say to us who
still survive : Love while ye may. This prodigy
indeed instructs us to taste the joys of life while
it is yet time."

Thus reflected this simple pagan. Upon this
subject he composed an elegy which by the greatest
of chances I unearthed in the public library at
Tarascon, on the binding of a Bible of the eleventh
century, catalogued Michel Chasles Collection F *n*
7439, 17⁹ *bis*. The precious leaf which had so far
escaped the notice of the learned, contains not fewer
than eighty-four lines in a fairly legible Merovingian
script probably dating from the seventh century.
The text begins with these words—

> Nunc piget ; et quaeris, quod non aut ista volontas
> Tunc fuit. . . .[1]

and finishes in this fashion—

> Stringamus maesti carminis obsequio.[2]

I shall not fail to publish the complete text so soon
as I have finished deciphering it. And I do not
doubt that Monsieur Leopold Delisle himself will
undertake to present this invaluable document to
the Academy of Inscriptions.

[1] Now regret rankles, and thou cravest that
Thou didst reject. . . .
[2] Weave we the tribute of a mournful song.

OUR LADY'S JUGGLER

TO GASTON PARIS

OUR LADY'S JUGGLER

I**N the days of King Louis there was a poor juggler in France, a native of Compiègne, Barnaby by name, who went about from town to town performing feats of skill and strength.**

On fair days he would unfold an old worn-out carpet in the public square, and when by means of a jovial address, which he had learned of a very ancient juggler, and which he never varied in the least, he had drawn together the children and loafers, he assumed extraordinary attitudes, and balanced a tin plate on the tip of his nose. At first the crowd would feign indifference.

But when, supporting himself on his hands face downwards, he threw into the air six copper balls, which glittered in the sunshine, and caught them again with his feet; or when throwing himself backwards until his heels and the nape of the neck met, giving his body the form of a perfect wheel, he would juggle in this posture with a dozen knives, a murmur of admiration would escape the spectators, and pieces of money rain down upon the carpet.

Nevertheless, like the majority of those who live by their wits, Barnaby of Compiègne had a great struggle to make a living.

Earning his bread in the sweat of his brow, he bore rather more than his share of the penalties consequent upon the misdoings of our father Adam.

Again, he was unable to work as constantly as he would have been willing to do. The warmth of the sun and the broad daylight were as necessary to enable him to display his brilliant parts as to the trees if flower and fruit should be expected of them. In winter time he was nothing more than a tree stripped of its leaves, and as it were dead. The frozen ground was hard to the juggler, and, like the grasshopper of which Marie de France tells us, the inclement season caused him to suffer both cold and hunger. But as he was simple-natured he bore his ills patiently.

He had never meditated on the origin of wealth, nor upon the inequality of human conditions. He believed firmly that if this life should prove hard, the life to come could not fail to redress the balance, and this hope upheld him. He did not resemble those thievish and miscreant Merry Andrews who sell their souls to the devil. He never blasphemed God's name; he lived uprightly, and although he had no wife of his own, he did not covet his neighbour's, since woman is ever the enemy of the strong man, as it appears by the history of Samson recorded in the Scriptures.

In truth, his was not a nature much disposed to carnal delights, and it was a greater deprivation to him to forsake the tankard than the Hebe who bore it. For whilst not wanting in sobriety, he was fond of a drink when the weather waxed hot. He was a worthy man who feared God, and was very devoted to the Blessed Virgin.

Never did he fail on entering a church to fall upon his knees before the image of the Mother of God, and offer up this prayer to her :

"Blessed Lady, keep watch over my life until it shall please God that I die, and when I am dead, ensure to me the possession of the joys of paradise."

NOW on a certain evening after a dreary wet day, as Barnaby pursued his road, sad and bent, carrying under his arm his balls and knives wrapped up in his old carpet, on the watch for some barn where, though he might not sup, he might sleep, he perceived on the road, going in the same direction as himself, a monk, whom he saluted courteously. And as they walked at the same rate they fell into conversation with one another.

"Fellow traveller," said the monk, "how comes it about that you are clothed all in green? Is it perhaps in order to take the part of a jester in some mystery play?"

"Not at all, good father," replied Barnaby. "Such as you see me, I am called Barnaby, and for my calling I am a juggler. There would be no pleasanter calling in the world if it would always provide one with daily bread."

"Friend Barnaby," returned the monk, "be careful what you say. There is no calling more pleasant than the monastic life. Those who lead it are occupied with the praises of God, the Blessed Virgin, and the saints ; and, indeed, the religious life is one ceaseless hymn to the Lord."

Barnaby replied—

"Good father, I own that I spoke like an ignorant man. Your calling cannot be in any respect compared to mine, and although there may be some merit in dancing with a penny balanced on a stick on the tip of one's nose, it is not a merit which comes within hail of your own. Gladly would I, like you, good father, sing my office day by day, and especially the office of the most Holy Virgin, to whom I have vowed a singular devotion. In order to embrace the monastic life I would willingly abandon the art by which from Soissons to Beauvais I am well known in upwards of six hundred towns and villages."

The monk was touched by the juggler's simplicity, and as he was not lacking in discernment, he at once recognized in Barnaby one of those men of whom it is said in the Scriptures : Peace on earth to men of good will. And for this reason he replied—

"Friend Barnaby, come with me, and I will have you admitted into the monastery of which I am Prior. He who guided St. Mary of Egypt in the desert set me upon your path to lead you into the way of salvation."

It was in this manner, then, that Barnaby became a monk. In the monastery into which he was received the religious vied with one another in the worship of the Blessed Virgin, and in her honour each employed all the knowledge and all the skill which God had given him.

The prior on his part wrote books dealing according to the rules of scholarship with the virtues of the Mother of God.

Brother Maurice, with a deft hand copied out these treatises upon sheets of vellum.

Brother Alexander adorned the leaves with delicate miniature paintings. Here were displayed the Queen of Heaven seated upon Solomon's throne, and while four lions were on guard at her feet, around the nimbus which encircled her head hovered seven doves, which are the seven gifts of the Holy Spirit, the gifts, namely, of Fear, Piety, Knowledge, Strength, Counsel, Understanding, and Wisdom. For her companions she had six virgins with hair of gold, namely, Humility, Prudence, Seclusion, Submission, Virginity, and Obedience.

At her feet were two little naked figures, perfectly white, in an attitude of supplication. These were souls imploring her all-powerful intercession for their soul's health, and we may be sure not imploring in vain.

Upon another page facing this, Brother Alexander represented Eve, so that the Fall and the Redemption could be perceived at one and the same time —Eve the Wife abased, and Mary the Virgin exalted.

Furthermore, to the marvel of the beholder, this book contained presentments of the Well of Living Waters, the Fountain, the Lily, the Moon, the Sun, and the Garden Enclosed of which the Song of Songs tells us, the Gate of Heaven and the City of God, and all these things were symbols of the Blessed Virgin.

Brother Marbode was likewise one of the most loving children of Mary.

He spent all his days carving images in stone, so that his beard, his eyebrows, and his hair were white with dust, and his eyes continually swollen and weeping; but his strength and cheerfulness were not diminished, although he was now well gone in years, and it was clear that the Queen of Paradise still cherished her servant in his old age.   Marbode represented her seated upon a throne, her brow encircled with an orb - shaped nimbus set with pearls.   And he took care that the folds of her dress should cover the feet of her, concerning whom the prophet declared : My beloved is as a garden enclosed.

Sometimes, too, he depicted her in the semblance of a child full of grace, and appearing to say, "Thou art my God, even from my mother's womb."

In the priory, moreover, were poets who composed hymns in Latin, both in prose and verse, in honour of the Blessed Virgin Mary, and amongst the company was even a brother from Picardy who sang the miracles of Our Lady in rhymed verse and in the vulgar tongue.

BEING a witness of this emulation in praise and the glorious harvest of their labours, Barnaby mourned his own ignorance and simplicity.

"Alas!" he sighed, as he took his solitary walk in the little shelterless garden of the monastery, "wretched wight that I am, to be unable, like my brothers, worthily to praise the Holy Mother of God, to whom I have vowed my whole heart's affection. Alas! alas! I am but a rough man and unskilled in the arts, and I can render you in service, blessed Lady, neither edifying sermons, nor treatises set out in order according to rule, nor ingenious paintings, nor statues truthfully sculptured, nor verses whose march is measured to the beat of feet. No gift have I, alas!"

After this fashion he groaned and gave himself up to sorrow. But one evening, when the monks were spending their hour of liberty in conversation, he heard one of them tell the tale of a religious man who could repeat nothing other than the Ave

Maria. This poor man was despised for his ignorance ; but after his death there issued forth from
his mouth five roses in honour of the five letters
of the name Mary (Marie), and thus his sanctity
was made manifest.

Whilst he listened to this narrative Barnaby
marvelled yet once again at the loving kindness of
the Virgin ; but the lesson of that blessed death
did not avail to console him, for his heart overflowed with zeal, and he longed to advance the
glory of his Lady, who is in heaven.

How to compass this he sought but could
find no way, and day by day he became the
more cast down, when one morning he awakened
filled full with joy, hastened to the chapel, and
remained there alone for more than an hour.
After dinner he returned to the chapel once
more.

And, starting from that moment, he repaired daily
to the chapel at such hours as it was deserted, and
spent within it a good part of the time which the
other monks devoted to the liberal and mechanical
arts. His sadness vanished, nor did he any longer
groan.

A demeanour so strange awakened the curiosity
of the monks.

These began to ask one another for what purpose

Brother Barnaby could be indulging so persistently in retreat.

The prior, whose duty it is to let nothing escape him in the behaviour of his children in religion, resolved to keep a watch over Barnaby during his withdrawals to the chapel. One day, then, when he was shut up there after his custom, the prior, accompanied by two of the older monks, went to discover through the chinks in the door what was going on within the chapel.

They saw Barnaby before the altar of the Blessed Virgin, head downwards, with his feet in the air, and he was juggling with six balls of copper and a dozen knives. In honour of the Holy Mother of God he was performing those feats, which aforetime had won him most renown. Not recognizing that the simple fellow was thus placing at the service of the Blessed Virgin his knowledge and skill, the two old monks exclaimed against the sacrilege.

The prior was aware how stainless was Barnaby's soul, but he concluded that he had been seized with madness. They were all three preparing to lead him swiftly from the chapel, when they saw the Blessed Virgin descend the steps of the altar and advance to wipe away with a fold of her azure robe the sweat which was dropping from her juggler's forehead.

Then the prior, falling upon his face upon the
pavement, uttered these words—

"Blessed are the simple-hearted, for they shall
see God."

"Amen!" responded the old brethren, and kissed
the ground.

THE MASS OF SHADOWS

TO MONSIEUR JEAN FRANÇOIS BLADE,
OF AGEN,

THE "PIOUS CHRONICLER" WHO HAS COLLECTED THE
POPULAR TALES OF GASCONY

THE MASS OF SHADOWS

THIS tale the sacristan of the church of St. Eulalie at Neuville d'Aumont told me, as we sat under the arbour of the White Horse, one fine summer evening, drinking a bottle of old wine to the health of the dead man, now very much at his ease, whom that very morning he had borne to the grave with full honours, beneath a pall powdered with smart silver tears.

"My poor father, who is dead" (it is the sacristan who is speaking), "was in his lifetime a gravedigger. He was of an agreeable disposition, the result, no doubt, of the calling he followed, for it has often been pointed out that people who work in cemeteries are of a jovial turn. Death has no terrors for them : they never give it a thought. I, for instance, Monsieur, enter a cemetery at night as little perturbed as though it were the arbour of the White Horse. And if by chance I meet with a ghost, I don't disturb myself in the least about it, for I reflect that he may just as likely have business of his own to attend to as I. I know the habits of the dead, and I know their character. Indeed, so far as that goes, I know things of which the priests themselves are ignorant. If I were to tell you all I have seen you would be astounded. But a still tongue makes a wise head, and my father, who, all the same, delighted in spinning a yarn, did not disclose a twentieth part of what he knew. To make up for this he often repeated the same stories, and to my knowledge he told the story of Catherine Fontaine at least a hundred times.

"Catherine Fontaine was an old maid whom he well remembered having seen when he was a mere child. I should not be surprised if there were still, perhaps, three old fellows in the district who could remember having heard folks speak of her, for she was very well known and of excellent reputation, although poor enough. She lived at the corner of the Rue aux Nonnes, in the turret which is still to be seen there, and which formed part of an old half-ruined mansion looking on to the garden of the Ursuline nuns. On that turret can still be traced certain figures and half-obliterated inscriptions. The late Curé of St. Eulalie, Monsieur Levasseur, asserted that there are the words in Latin, *Love is stronger than death*, 'which is to be understood,' so he would add, 'of divine love.'

"Catherine Fontaine lived by herself in this tiny apartment. She was a lacemaker. You know, of course, that the lace made in our part of the world was formerly held in high esteem. No one knew anything of her relatives or friends. It was reported that when she was eighteen years of age she had loved the young Chevalier d'Aumont-Cléry, and been secretly affianced to him. But decent folk didn't believe a word of it, and said it was nothing but a tale which had been concocted because Catherine Fontaine's demeanour was that of a lady rather than of a working woman, and because, moreover, she possessed beneath her white locks the remains of great beauty. Her expression was sorrowful, and on one finger she wore one of those rings fashioned by the goldsmith into the semblance of two tiny hands clasped together. In former days folks were accustomed to exchange such rings at their betrothal ceremony. I am sure you know the sort of thing I mean.

"Catherine Fontaine lived a saintly life. She spent a great deal of time in the churches, and every morning, whatever might be the weather, she went to assist at the six o'clock Mass at St. Eulalie.

"Now one December night, whilst she was abed in her little chamber, she was awakened by the sound of bells, and nothing doubting that they were ringing for the first Mass, the pious woman dressed herself and came downstairs and out into

the street. The night was so obscure that not even
the walls of the houses were visible, and not a ray
of light shone from the murky sky. And such was
the silence amid this black darkness, that there
was not even the sound of a distant dog barking,
and a feeling of aloofness from every living creature
was perceptible. But Catherine Fontaine knew
well every single stone she stepped on, and as she
could have found her way to the church with her
eyes shut, she reached without difficulty the corner
of the Rue aux Nonnes and the Rue de la Paroisse,
where the timbered house stands with the tree of
Jesse carved on one of its massive beams. When
she reached this spot she perceived that the church
doors were open, and that a great light was stream-
ing out from the wax tapers. She resumed her
journey, and when she had passed through the
porch she found herself in the midst of a vast congregation which entirely filled the church. But
she did not recognize any of the worshippers, and
was surprised to observe that all these people were
dressed in velvets and brocades, with feathers in
their hats, and that they wore swords in the fashion
of days gone by. Here were gentlemen who carried
tall canes with gold knobs, and ladies with lace
caps fastened with coronet-shaped combs. Cheva-
liers of the Order of St. Louis extended their
hands to these ladies, who concealed behind their

fans painted faces, of which only the powdered
brow and the patch at the corner of the eye were
visible ! And all of them proceeded to take up
their places without the slightest sound, and as
they moved neither the sound of their footsteps on
the pavement nor the rustle of their garments could
be heard. The lower places were filled with a
crowd of young artisans in brown jackets, dimity
breeches, and blue stockings, with their arms round
the waists of very pretty blushing girls who lowered
their eyes. Near the holy water stoups peasant
women, in scarlet petticoats and laced bodices, sat
upon the ground as immovable as domestic animals,
whilst young lads, standing up behind them, stared
out from wide-open eyes and twirled their hats
round and round on their fingers, and all these
silent countenances seemed centred irremovably on
one and the same thought, at once sweet and
sorrowful. On her knees, in her accustomed place,
Catherine Fontaine saw the priest advance towards
the altar, preceded by two servers. She recognized
neither priest nor clerks. The Mass began. It was
a silent Mass, during which neither the sound of
the moving lips nor the tinkle of the bell, vainly
swung to and fro, was audible. Catherine Fontaine
felt that she was under the observation and the
influence also of her mysterious neighbour, and
when, scarcely turning her head, she stole a glance

at him, she recognized the young Chevalier
d'Aumont-Cléry who had once loved her, and who
had been dead for five-and-forty years. She recognized him by a small mark which he had over the
left ear, and, above all, by the shadow which his
long black eyelashes cast upon his cheeks. He
was dressed in his hunting clothes, scarlet with gold
lace, the very clothes he wore that day when he met
her in St. Leonard's Wood, begged her for a drink,
and stole a kiss. He had preserved his youth and
his good looks. When he smiled he still displayed
magnificent teeth. Catherine said to him in an
undertone—

"'Monseigneur, you who were my friend, and to
whom in days gone by I gave all that a girl holds
most dear, may God keep you in His grace! O,
that he would at length inspire me with regret for
the sin I committed in yielding to you; for it is a
fact that, though my hair is white and I approach
my end, I have not yet repented of having loved
you. But, dear dead friend and noble seigneur,
tell me, who are these folk, habited after the antique
fashion, who are here assisting at this silent
Mass?'

"The Chevalier d'Aumont-Cléry replied in a
voice feebler than a breath, but none the less crystal
clear—

"'Catherine, these men and women are souls

from purgatory who have grieved God by sinning as we ourselves sinned through love of the creature, but who are not on that account cast off by God, inasmuch as their sin, like ours, was not deliberate.

"'Whilst, separated from those they loved upon earth, they are purified in the cleansing fires of purgatory, they suffer the pangs of absence, which is for them the most cruel of tortures. They are so unhappy that an angel from heaven takes pity upon their love-torment. By the permission of the Most High, for one hour in the night, he reunites each year lover to loved in their parish church, where they are permitted to assist at the Mass of Shadows, hand clasped in hand. These are the facts. If it has been granted to me to see thee here before thy death, Catherine, it is a boon which has been bestowed by God's special permission.'

"And Catherine Fontaine answered him—

"'I would die gladly enough, dear, dead lord, if I might recover the beauty that was mine when I gave you to drink in the forest.'

"Whilst they conversed thus under their breath, a very old canon was taking the collection and proffering to the worshippers a great copper dish, wherein they let fall, each in his turn, ancient coins which have long since ceased to pass current : écus

of six livres, florins, ducats and ducatoons, jaco-
buses and rose-nobles, and the pieces fell silently
into the dish. When at length it was placed before
the Chevalier, he dropped into it a louis which
made no more sound than had the other pieces of
gold and silver.

"Then the old canon stopped before Catherine
Fontaine, who fumbled in her pocket without being
able to find a farthing. Then, being unwilling to
allow the dish to pass without an offering from herself, she slipped from her finger the ring which the
Chevalier had given her the day before his death,
and cast it into the copper bowl. As the golden
ring fell, a sound like the heavy clang of a bell rang
out, and on the stroke of this reverberation the
Chevalier, the canon, the celebrant, the servers,
the ladies and their cavaliers, the whole assembly
vanished utterly; the candles guttered out, and
Catherine Fontaine was left alone in the darkness."

Having concluded his narrative after this fashion,
the sacristan drank a long draught of wine, remained
pensive a moment, and then resumed his talk in
these words :—

"I have told you this tale exactly as my father
has told it to me over and over again, and I believe

that it is authentic, because it agrees in all respects with what I have myself observed of the manners and customs peculiar to those who have passed away. I have associated a good deal with the dead ever since my childhood, and I know that they are accustomed to return to what they have loved.

"It is on this account that the miserly dead wander at night in the neighbourhood of the treasures they concealed during their lifetime. They keep a strict watch over their gold; but the trouble they give themselves, far from being of service to them, turns to their disadvantage; and it is not at all a rare thing to come upon money buried in the ground on digging in a place haunted by a ghost. In the same way deceased husbands come by night to harass their wives who have made a second matrimonial venture, and I could easily name several who have kept a better watch over their wives since death than ever they did while living.

"That sort of thing is blameworthy, for in all fairness the dead have no business to stir up jealousies. Still I do but tell you what I have observed myself. It is a matter to take into account if one marries a widow. Besides, the tale I have told you is vouched for in the manner following:

"The morning after that extraordinary night Catherine Fontaine was discovered dead in her chamber. And the beadle attached to St. Eulalie found in the copper bowl used for the collection a gold ring with two clasped hands. Besides, I'm not the kind of man to make jokes. Suppose we order another bottle of wine ? . . ."

LESLIE WOOD

TO THE COMTESSE DE MARTEL-JANVILLE

LESLIE WOOD

THERE was music and private theatricals at Madame N——'s reception in the Boulevard Malesherbes.

Whilst on the outskirts of a display of bare shoulders the younger men at the doorway were suffocating in the stifling, scented air, we older guests, not without grumbling, were keeping ourselves cool in a little *salon* from which we could see nothing, and to which the voice of Mademoiselle Réjane only penetrated like the slightly metallic sound of a dragon-fly's flight. From time to time we could hear the laughter and applause burst forth in the sweltering room, and we were disposed to extend a mild tolerance to the entertainment we did not share. We were exchanging fairly amusing trivialities, when one of the company, a genial deputy, Monsieur B——, remarked—

"Did you know that Wood was here?"

At this statement each in turn exclaimed—

"Wood? Leslie Wood? It's impossible. It is ten years since he was seen in Paris. Nobody knows what's become of him."

"The story goes that he has established a black republic on the shores of the Victoria Nyanza."

"What a tale! You know, of course, that he is fabulously wealthy, and that he is a past master in achieving the impossible. Well, he is living in Ceylon, in a fairy palace, in the midst of enchanted gardens, where the bayadères never cease dancing night and day."

"How can any one believe such balderdash? The truth is, that Leslie Wood has gone off with a Bible and a carbine to convert the Zulus."

Monsieur B—— interrupted in an undertone—

"There he is; there, do you see?"

And he drew our attention by a slight movement of the head and eyes to a man leaning against the doorway, dominating by his lofty stature the heads of the crowd huddled in front of him. He seemed engrossed in the performance.

That athletic carriage, the ruddy face with the white whiskers, the penetrating eyes and calm gaze, they could belong to no one else but Leslie Wood.

Recalling the inimitable letters which for ten years he contributed to the *World*, I said to Monsieur B——

"That man is the foremost journalist of our time."

"You may possibly be right," replied B——. "At any rate, I am ready to assert that for twenty

years past no one has known Europe as thoroughly
as Leslie Wood."

Baron Moïse, who was following our talk, shook
his head.

"You don't know the real Wood. I know him
myself, though. He was before all things a financier.
He had a better grasp of the money market than
any one I know. What are you laughing at,
Princess?"

Lolling expansively on the sofa, and in gloomy
depression at being unable to smoke a cigarette,
the Princess Zévorine had smiled.

"You neither of you understand Mr. Wood—
neither of you," she said. "He was always a
mystic and a lover, never anything else."

"I can't agree to that," replied Baron Moïse.
"But I should be very glad to know where this
devil of a fellow has been spending the best ten
years of his life."

"And at what period do you place those best ten
years of life?"

"Between the fiftieth and sixtieth years; a man's
position is made by then, and he has nothing to do
but enjoy his existence."

"Baron, you can question Wood himself. He
is coming towards us."

The applause, this time rising to a furious pitch
like the fall of a heavy body or the banging of

doors, announced the close of the performance. The black-coated contingent leaving the doorways clear overflowed into the smaller *salon*, and as the company made their way in couples in the direction of the buffet, Leslie Wood approached us.

He shook hands with undemonstrative cordiality.

"An apparition! an apparition!" exclaimed Baron Moïse.

"Oh!" rejoined Wood, "one can't reappear from any very remote quarter. The world is small."

"Do you know what the Princess is saying about you, my dear Wood? She declares that you are nothing but a mystic. Now is that true?"

"Well it depends on what you mean by mystic."

"The word is self-explanatory. A mystic is one who is preoccupied with the concerns of the next world. Now you are too well acquainted with the affairs of this world to trouble yourself about the next."

At these words Wood slightly contracted his eyebrows.

"You are quite in the wrong, Moïse. The affairs of the other world are of far, far greater importance than those of the world we live in, Moïse."

"What a man he is, this good Wood of ours!" exclaimed the Baron, with a sneer. "He is positively witty!"

The Princess replied very seriously—

" Mr. Wood, tell me that you are not witty. I thoroughly detest witty men."

Upon this she rose, and said—

" Mr. Wood, will you take me to the buffet ? "

An hour later, when Monsieur G—— was holding both men and women spell-bound with his songs, I came across Leslie Wood and the Princess Zévorine again, alone in front of the deserted buffet.

The Princess was speaking with almost vehement enthusiasm of Count Tolstoi, whose friend she was. She described this great man who had descended to the lowliest life, donning the dress, and with it the spirit, of the moujik, and using the hands which had indited literary masterpieces in the manufacture of shoes for the poor.

To my great surprise, Wood was expressing approbation of a kind of life so completely opposed to common sense. In his slightly panting voice, to which the beginnings of asthma had given a singular sweetness, he said—

" Yes, Tolstoi is right. The whole of philosophy is contained in that phrase : ' May the will of God be done !' He has realized that all the woes of humanity are the outcome of the exercise of human will as distinct from the will divine. My only fear is that he may impair so noble a doctrine by fantastic and extravagant additions."

I

"Oh!" returned the Princess in a subdued voice, and hesitating a little, "the Count's teaching is only extravagant upon one point; that is, in inculcating the extension of the rights and duties of husbands to an extremely advanced period of their lives, and imposing on the saints of these latter days the fruitful old age of the patriarchs."

Wood, himself elderly, replied with a restrained exaltation—

"And that again is excellent, very saintly even. Physical and natural love is becoming to all God's creatures, and so long as it does not involve either dissension or restlessness, it maintains that divine simplicity, that saintly fleshliness without which there is no salvation. Asceticism is nothing but pride and rebellion. We must always bear in mind the example of that holy man Boaz, and let us remember that the Bible calls love the bread of old age."

Then, all of a sudden, transported, illuminated, transfigured, ecstatic, and invoking with eyes and arms and his whole soul some invisible presence, he murmured—

"Annie! Annie! Annie, my best beloved, it is true, is it not, that our Lord desires his saints, whilst they are men and women, to love one another humbly, even as the beasts of the field?"

Upon this he fell exhausted into an arm-chair.

A terrific inhalation shook his broad chest, and in this condition his appearance was fuller of vitality than ever, like those machines that appear more formidable when they are out of gear. The Princess Zévorine, without any show of astonishment, wiped his forehead with her handkerchief and gave him a glass of water, which he drank.

For my part I was dumfounded. In this clairvoyant I was unable to recognize the man who in his study, littered with blue-books, had so many times conversed with me with the utmost clear-headedness upon Oriental affairs, the Treaty of Frankfort, and critical situations on the money market. As I allowed the Princess to observe my uneasiness, she said, with a shrug of the shoulders—

"It is easy to see you are French! You look upon every one as a madman who does not think exactly what you think yourself. You need not be uneasy; our friend Mr. Wood is level-headed enough, perfectly level-headed. Let us go and listen to G——.

When I had conducted the Princess to the principal *salon*, I prepared to leave. In the ante-chamber I found Wood putting on his overcoat. He did not appear to feel any ill effects from his attack.

"My dear fellow," he said, "I think we are neighbours. I suppose you are still living on the Quai Malaquais, and I have taken up my quarters

in a hotel in the Rue des Saints Pères. In dry
weather like this it is a pleasure to go on foot. If
you are willing we will stroll along together and
chat."

I agreed readily. On the doorstep he offered
me a cigar, and held out a pocket electric torch
for me to light it by.

"I find it very convenient," he said, and proceeded to explain the principle of it very lucidly.

I recognized the Wood of old times again. We
moved on perhaps a hundred paces along the street
chatting on indifferent subjects. Then suddenly
my companion put his hand quietly on my
shoulder.

"My dear friend," he began, "some of the
things I said this evening cannot have failed to
surprise you. You would probably like me to
explain them."

"I was intensely interested, my dear Wood,
pray do."

"I will do so willingly. I have the greatest
admiration of your character. We may not regard
life from the same point of view. But you are
not one of those who repel an idea because it is
new, and that is a disposition sufficiently rare, in
France especially."

"I fancy, however, my dear Wood, that for
liberty of thought——"

"Oh! no, you are not, like the English, a race of theologians. But enough of that. I want to tell you in as few words as possible the history of my convictions. When you knew me fifteen years ago I was the correspondent of the London *World*. With us journalism is a more lucrative profession, and is held in higher esteem than with you. My appointment was a good one, and I fancy I reaped the greatest possible advantages from it. I am familiar with business transactions, and I carried through some very profitable ones, and in a few years I achieved two very desirable things : influence and fortune. You are aware that I am a practical man.

"I have never worked without a goal in view. And, above all things, I aimed at attaining the supreme goal of life. Fairly exhaustive theological studies undertaken in my youth had convinced me that that goal lay outside the sphere of this terrestrial life. But I was yet in doubt as to the practical means of attaining it. As a result, I suffered cruelly. Uncertainty is absolutely insupportable to a man of my temperament.

"In this state of mind I turned my attention seriously to the psychical researches of Sir William Crookes, one of the most distinguished members of our Royal Society. I knew him personally, and needed no assurance that he was both a man of learning and a gentleman. He was at that time giving his attention to the case of a young woman endowed with psychic powers of an altogether uncommon nature, and, like Saul of old, he was fortunate enough to evoke the presence of an indisputable disembodied spirit.

"A charming woman, who had passed through the experience of earthly life and was now living the life beyond the tomb, lent herself to the experiments of the eminent spiritualist, and submitted to every test he could exact from her within the limits of decorum. I considered that investigations such as this, bearing on the point at which terrestrial existence borders on extra-terrestrial existence, would lead me, if I followed them step by step, to the discovery of that which it is above all necessary to know, that is to say, the true aim of life. But it was not long before I was disappointed in my hopes. The researches of my respected friend, although conducted with a precision which left nothing to be desired, did not result in a theological and moral conviction sufficiently unequivocal.

" Moreover, Sir William was suddenly deprived of the co-operation of the incomparable dead lady who had so graciously attended several of his spiritualistic séances.

" Discouraged by the incredulity of the public,

and irritated by the sallies of his colleagues, he ceased to give any information relative to his psychic experiences. I communicated my discomfiture to the Reverend Mr. B——, with whom I had been on friendly terms from the time of his return from South Africa, where he had laboured as an evangelist in a devoted and systematic fashion truly worthy of old England.

"Mr. B—— is, of all men, the one who has at all times exercised the most powerful and decisive influence over me."

"He is very intellectual, then ?" I asked.

"His knowledge of doctrine is profound," replied Wood. "But better than all else he has a strong character, and you are aware, my dear fellow, that it is by force of character that men are swayed. My mischances occasioned no surprise to him ; he attributed them to my lack of method, and, above all, to the pitiable moral infirmity I had shown on this occasion.

"'Scientific experiments,' he declared, 'can never lead to discoveries in any other domain than that of science. How is it you did not understand this ? Leslie Wood, you have been strangely heedless and frivolous. The Apostle Paul has told us that the Spirit searcheth all things. If we would discover spiritual truths we must set our feet on the spiritual path.'

"These words produced a profound impression on me.

"'How then,' I asked, 'shall I enter on the spiritual path?'

"'Poverty and simplicity must be your guides!' Mr. B—— replied. 'Sell your goods and give the purchase money to the poor. You are renowned. Conceal yourself. Pray, and devote yourself to works of charity. Put on a spirit of simplicity and a pure soul and you will attain truth.'

"I resolved to follow out these precepts to the letter. I sent in my resignation as correspondent to the *World*. I realized my investments, which were in great part in commercial enterprises, and, fearing to repeat the sin of Ananias and Sapphira, I conducted this delicate operation in such a way as not to risk the loss of a penny of the capital which was no longer my own. Baron Moïse, who kept an eye on my negotiations, conceived an almost religious reverence for my financial genius. By direction of Mr. B——, I handed over to the treasurer of the *Evangelical Society* the sums I had realized, and when I expressed to that eminent theologian my delight at being poor—

"'Have a care,' said he, 'that in your poverty you do not indulge in exaltation at your prowess. It will serve you but ill to strip yourself outwardly if within your own breast you cherish a golden idol. Be humble!'"

Leslie Wood had reached this point in his narrative when we arrived at the Pont Royal. The Seine, upon whose surface the lights threw flickering reflections, flowed beneath the arches with a dull moan.

"I shall have to cut my story short," Wood began once more. "Each episode of my new life would occupy a whole night to recount. Mr. B——, to whom I was as obedient as a child, sent me to the Basutos, commissioned to fight against the slave trade. There I lived under a tent alone with that hardy bedfellow whose name is danger, and through fever and drought became aware of the presence of God.

"At the end of five years Mr. B—— recalled me to England. On the steamer I met a young girl. What a haunting face she had! She was a vision a thousand times more radiant than the phantom presence which appeared to Sir William Crookes!

"She was the orphan daughter of a colonel in the Indian army and she was poor. She had no particular beauty of features. Her pale complexion and emaciated face indicated suffering; but her eyes expressed all that one can imagine of heaven; her body seemed to glow gently with an inward light. How I loved her! At sight of her I fathomed the hidden meaning of all creation! That simple young girl with one glance revealed to me the secret of the harmony of the spheres!

"Ah! she was simple, very simple, my monitress, my well-loved lady, sweet Annie Fraser! In her translucent soul I could read the sympathy she felt for me. One night, one serene night, when we were alone together on the deck of the ship in the presence of the seraphic company of the stars, which throbbed in chorus in the sky, I took her hand and said—

"'Annie Fraser, I love you. I believe that it would be good for us both for you to become my wife, but I am debarred from planning my own future in order that God may dispose of it as He sees fit. May it be His will to unite us! I have surrendered my own will into the hands of Mr. B——. When we reach England we will go together in search of him; will you, Annie Fraser? And if he gives his sanction we will marry.'

"She gave her consent. For the remainder of the voyage we read the Bible together.

"Immediately on our arrival in London I accompanied my fellow passenger to Mr. B——'s, and told him what the love of this young girl meant to me, and with what clear insight it inspired me.

"Mr. B—— gazed for a long time on her with kindliness.

"'You may marry,' he said at length. 'The Apostle Paul has declared that the husband is sanctified by the wife, and the wife by the husband. But let your union resemble those held in honour amongst Christians in the primitive Church! Let it remain purely spiritual, and see that the angel's sword lies between you in your bed. Go, now, and remain humble and secluded, and let not the world hear your name.'

"I married Annie Fraser, and I need scarcely tell you that we complied rigidly with the condition imposed on us by Mr. B——. For four years I delighted in that brotherly and sisterly union.

"By grace of simple little Annie Fraser I advanced in the knowledge of God. There was nothing now that could cause us suffering.

"Annie was ill, and her strength declined, and we repeated joyfully in union, 'May the will of God be done on earth as it is in heaven!'

"After four years of this life together, there came a day, a Christmas day, when Mr. B—— summoned me to him.

"'Leslie Wood,' he said, 'I have put you to the proof for your soul's sake. But it would be to fall into papistical error to believe that the union of His creatures after the flesh is displeasing to God. Twice He blessed both animals and mankind in pairs, in the earthly Paradise, and in the ark of Noah. Go, and live henceforth with your wife, Annie Fraser, as a husband with his wife.'

"When I arrived home, Annie, my well-loved Annie, was dead. . . .

"I own my weakness. It was with my lips and not with my heart that I pronounced the words, 'O God, Thy will be done!' and thinking upon Mr. B——'s tardy removal of the restrictions upon our love, I felt my mouth full of bitterness, and as it were ashes in my heart.

"So it was with a forlorn soul that I knelt down at the foot of the bed where, beneath a cross of roses, silent and white and with the faint violets of death on her cheeks, my Annie slept her last sleep.

"O thou of little faith! thou didst bid her adieu and remain a whole week plunged in barren sorrow that approached despair. How much rather shouldst thou, on the contrary, have rejoiced, both in body and soul! . . .

"On the night of the eighth day, as I was weeping, my forehead bowed upon the cold and empty bed, I had a sudden conviction that the beloved was near me in my chamber.

"Nor was I deceived. When I raised my head

I saw Annie, smiling and radiant, holding out her arms to me. But how find words for what remains to tell? How express the ineffable? And is it permissible to reveal such mysteries of love?

"Clearly when Mr. B—— said to me, 'Live with Annie as a husband with his wife!' he knew that love is stronger than death.

"Learn, then, my friend, that from that hour of forgiveness and joy my Annie has returned nightly to my side distilling celestial odours."

He spoke with appalling exaltation.

We had slackened our pace. He stopped in front of a hotel of Moorish exterior.

"This is where I live," he said. "Do you see that window on the second floor with the light in it? She is waiting for me."

He left me abruptly.

Eight days later I learned from the newspapers of the sudden death of Leslie Wood, former correspondent of the *World*.

GESTAS

TO CHARLES MAURRAS

GESTAS

"' Gestas,' dixt li Signor, 'entrez en Paradis.'"

"Gestas, dans nos anciens mystères, c'est le nom du larron crucifié à la droite de Jésus-Christ " (Augustin Thierry, *la Rédemption de Larmor*).[1]

FOLKS say that we have amongst us at this very day a sad rogue named Gestas, who writes the sweetest songs in the world. It was written on his flat-featured face that he would be a sinner after the flesh, and towards evening evil exultation shines in his green eyes. He is no longer young. The protuberances on his skull have taken on the lustre of copper ; the long hair falling about his neck has taken a greenish tinge. Nevertheless he is ingenuous, and has kept fast hold on the naive faith of his childhood. When he is not in hospital he occupies a little room in some squalid hotel between the Panthéon and the Jardin des

---

[1] "' Gestas,' said the Lord, 'enter into Paradise.'"

"Gestas, in our ancient mystery plays, was the name of the thief who was crucified on the right hand of Jesus Christ " (Augustin Thierry, *The Redemption of Larmor*).

Plantes. There, in the old impoverished quarter, every stone is familiar with his tread, the gloomy byways are tolerant of him, and one of these narrow lanes is entirely after his own heart; for, lined though it is with dram shops and boosing kens, it boasts on the corner of one of the houses an image of the Virgin in a blue niche behind bars. Of an evening he progresses from café to café, and at station after station, with pious orderliness, he takes his beer or his spirits : the exacting duties of the devotee of debauchery call for method and regularity. The night is far gone when, without knowing how, he once more reaches his den, and by a daily miracle discovers the sacking bed, upon which he falls fully dressed. There with clenched fists he sleeps the sleep of the vagabond and the child. But that sleep is brief.

As soon as dawn casts its pale radiance upon the window, and between the curtains darts its luminous shafts into the attic, Gestas opens his eyes, rises, shakes himself like an ownerless dog awakened by a kick, hurries down the long, spiral staircase, and once more sets his eyes delightedly on the street, the kind street which is so indulgent to the vices of the lowly and the poor. His eyelids wink at the clear light of the early morning; the nostrils, which recall Silenus, inhale the clean air. Vigorous and upright, one leg stiffened by rheuma-

tism of long standing, he goes on his way leaning
on his dog-wood stick, the ferrule of which he has
worn out with twenty years of wandering. But in
his nocturnal adventures he has never lost either
his pipe or his stick. And at the beginning of the
day his appearance is that of a man perfectly simple
and perfectly happy. Which is what he actually is.
His greatest joy in life, which he buys at the
sacrifice of sleep, is to go from bar to bar in the
morning drinking white wine with the workmen.
It is an innocent sort of tippling: the trans-
parent wine, in the pale light of early morning,
amongst the white blouses of the masons; there
you have a symphony in whites which enchants
this soul, of which vice has not yet subdued the
candour.

Now one spring morning when he had sauntered
in this fashion from his lodging as far as *The Little
Moor*, Gestas had the satisfaction of seeing the door,
over which appeared a Saracen's head in cast iron,
gay with paint, thrown open as he came up, and so he
reached the tin counter in the company of friends with
whom he had no acquaintance: a gang of workmen
from La Creuse, who clinked their glasses, talked
of their own part of the country, and indulged in
boasting after the manner of the twelve peers of
Charlemagne. They drank a glass and cracked a
crust; when one of them thought of a good thing

he laughed very loudly at it, and so that his comrades might understand it the better gave them a good thump or two on the back with his fist. The older men, however, dispatched their potations slowly and silently. When these had all departed to their work, Gestas, the last left, quitted *The Little Moor* and made his way to *The Juicy Quince*, with the lance-headed railings of which he was familiar. Here, again, in excellent company, he had a drink, and even offered a glass to two mistrustful but mild guardians of the peace. After this he visited a third bar, the ancient wrought-iron sign of which represents two little men staggering under an enormous bunch of grapes, and there he was served by the lovely Madame Trubert, famous all the quarter through for her prudence, her strength, and her jollity. Then as he neared the fortifications he had yet another drink at the distillery where, in the shadow, the gleaming copper taps of the barrels attract the eye; and still another at the general shop where the green shutters were still fast closed between the two boxes of laurels; after which he returned to the most populous districts and ordered *vermouth* and a sort of mixture of dregs in various cafés. Eight o'clock struck. He walked very erect, with a steady, rigid, solemn gait; he was astonished when women, running to buy provisions, with bare head and their hair twisted in a knot low

on the neck, ran against him with their heavy
baskets, or when he came into collision with some
small girl grasping an enormous loaf in her arms.
Still, at times, if he crossed the road the milkman's
cart, with its clinking, rattling tin cans, would pull
up so close to him that he could feel the horse's
warm breath on his cheek. But he continued his
way unhasting and careless of the imprecations of
the rustic milk-vendor. His gait, secure of support from his dog-wood stick, was calm and haughty.
But internally the old man was staggering. Nothing was left of his early morning gaiety. The
lark, whose joyous trills had thrilled through him
with his earliest sips of the pale-hued wine, had
sped away at a single flight, and now his soul was a
murky rookery, where crows croaked hoarsely upon
inky trees. He was mortally sad. A great disgust of himself welled up in his heart. The voice
of his repentance, his shame, cried out in him :
"Hog, hog! What a hog you are!" And he
marvelled at that clear, angry voice, that superb
angel's voice, which spoke mysteriously within
himself, repeating : "Hog! hog! What a hog
you are!" A yearning desire for innocence and
purity woke in him. He wept ; great tears fell
down on his goat-like beard. He wept over himself. Obedient to the words of his Master, who
said, "Weep for yourselves and for your children,

O daughters of Jerusalem," he shed the bitter
dew from his downcast eyes upon the body he had
delivered up to the seven deadly sins, and upon
the obscene fancies born of his drunkenness. The
faith of his childhood revived in him, and spread
out fresh vigorous tendrils. From his lips pathetic
prayers flowed forth. He said under his breath :
" O God, grant me to become once more even as
the little child which once was I ! " At the moment
he offered up this simple petition he realized that
he was standing under a church porch.

It was an old church, once white and comely
beneath its lacework of stone, which time and the
hand of man had marred. Now it had become as
black as the Shulamite, and its beauty could only
appeal to the hearts of poets ; it was a church
" little and poor and old," like the mother of
François Villon, who perchance in her day came to
kneel in its precincts, and saw on the walls, nowadays whitewashed, that painted paradise, the harps
of which she believed she could hear, and that
inferno where the damned suffered fiery torment,
which caused the worthy soul to be much afraid.
Gestas entered into the House of God. He saw
no one within, not even any one to offer him holy
water, not even a poor woman like the mother of
François Villon. Ranged in seemly order in the
nave, a congregation of chairs alone bore witness to

the faith of the parishioners, and seemed to sustain public worship.

In the cool, moist shade afforded by the vaulting Gestas turned to his right towards the aisle where, close to the porch, before a statue of the Virgin, a pyramidal frame of iron displayed its pointed teeth, on which, however, not a single taper now burned. Then as he gazed on the image, white, pink, and blue in colour, smiling from the midst of little gold and silver hearts hung up as votive offerings, he bent his stiff old legs, wept tears like St. Peter, and sobbed out tender, disconnected words : " Holy Virgin, Mother, Mary, Mary, your child, your child, Mother ! " But very speedily he rose up again, took several rapid steps, and stopped in front of a confessional. Framed of oak, darkened by the passage of time, oiled as are the beams of an olive press, this confessional had the irreproachable, homely, intimate appearance of an old linen cupboard. On its panels religious symbols carved in shell-like lozenges and rusticated work called up the memory of the townswomen of the olden time, who had come hither to bow their caps with lofty erections of lace and lave their house-wifely souls in this type of the cleansing piscina. Where they had set their knees Gestas set his, and with lips close up to the wooden grating called in a hushed voice : " Father ! father ! " As no one answered his call he knocked very gently with his finger on the wicket.

"Father! father!"

He wiped his eyes so as to see better through the holes in the grating, and thought he could make out through the dimness the white surplice of a priest.

He repeated—

"Father! father! pray listen to me. I am in need of confession, I must cleanse my soul; it is black and dirty; it disgusts me; it turns my stomach. Quick, father, the bath of repentance, the bath of pardon, the bath of Jesus. At the thought of my impurities my heart comes into my mouth, and I am ready to spew with disgust at my uncleanness. The bath, the bath of cleansing!"

Then he waited. Now fancying he perceived a hand, which made a sign to him from the depths of the confessional, now failing to discover in the alcove anything more than an empty seat, a long time passed. He remained motionless, his knees glued to the wooden step, his gaze intent on the wicket, whence he awaited the outpouring of pardon, peace, refreshment, health, innocence, reconciliation with God and himself, heavenly joy, submission to the divine love, the sovereign good. At intervals he murmured tender supplications—

"Monsieur le curé, father, monsieur le curé!

I thirst! give me to drink, give me that which is yours to give, the water of innocence, a white robe, and wings for my poor soul. Give me penitence and pardon!"

Receiving no reply, he knocked still harder at the grating, and said aloud—

"Confession, I beg of you!"

At last he lost patience, and rising, showered heavy blows with his dog-wood stick on the walls of the confessional, shouting—

"Ho, there, monsieur le curé! Ho, there, monsieur le vicaire!"

And in proportion as he raised his voice he knocked more loudly. The blows fell furiously on the confessional, causing clouds of dust to arise from it, and only evoking in reply to his violence the vibration of its worm-eaten old planks.

The verger, who was sweeping out the sacristy, ran forward with his sleeves turned up on hearing the noise. When he saw the man with the stick he stopped short for a moment, and then advanced towards him with the cautious reserve common to the officials who have grown white in the service of this lowliest of police. Arrived within earshot he demanded—

"What is it you want?"

"I want to confess."

"Folks don't come to confess at an hour like this."

"I want to confess."

"Be off with you!"

"I want to see the curé."

"For what purpose?"

"To make my confession."

"The curé can't be seen just now."

"The senior vicaire, then."

"Nor he either. Now off you go."

"The second vicaire, the third vicaire, the fourth vicaire, the youngest vicaire."

"Be off with you."

"Ah, then! would you let me die unshriven? It's worse than it was in '93, it seems! . . . Any little vicaire. How will it hurt you if I make my confession to some little vicaire not any taller than my arm? Take word to some priest that he must come to hear my confession. I'll undertake to disclose to him a batch of sins rarer, more extraordinary, more interesting, you may take my word for it, than all those his chattering women penitents can trot out before him. You can tell him that he is wanted for a really fine confession."

"Get away now!"

"But won't you understand, you old Barabbas, you? I tell you that I wish to reconcile myself with the good God—by God, I do!"

Although he did not rejoice in the majestic stature of the verger of a rich parish, this official staff-bearer was vigorous enough. He took our poor Gestas by the shoulders and hurled him outside the doors.

Gestas, once in the street, had only one idea in his brain, which was to get back into the church by one of the side doors, so as, if possible, to steal a march on the verger from behind, and perhaps lay hands on some underling vicaire who would consent to hear his confession.

Unhappily for the success of this manœuvre, the church was surrounded on all sides by old houses, and Gestas was soon hopelessly entangled, without hope of delivery, in an inextricable maze of streets, lanes, courts, and alleys.

Amongst them, however, he discovered a wine merchant's, and there the poor penitent tried to find consolation in absinthe. He managed to do so. But a fresh fit of repentance soon overtook him. And it is this which supports his friends in the hope that he will win salvation. He has faith—simple, firm, childlike faith. It is works alone which he is lacking in. Nevertheless there is no need to despair of him, since he himself never despairs.

Without entering on the difficulties as to predestination—and they are not inconsiderable—nor weighing the opinions expressed on this subject by St. Augustine, Gottschalk, the Albigenses, the Wycliffites, the Hussites, Luther, Calvin, Jansenius, and the great Arnaud, one may venture to believe that Gestas is predestined to eternal felicity.

"Gestas." said the Lord. "enter into Paradise."

THE MANUSCRIPT OF A VILLAGE DOCTOR

TO MARCEL SCHWOB

THE MANUSCRIPT OF A VILLAGE DOCTOR

DOCTOR H——, who recently died at Servigny (Aisne), where he had practised medicine for more than forty years, left behind him a journal never intended for the public eye. I should not feel justified in publishing the manuscript *in extenso*, nor even in printing fragments of any considerable length, although, like Monsieur Taine, there is a large number of persons nowadays of the opinion that it is above all things desirable to print and circulate what was never planned for publication. Whatever these worthy folk may say, the fact that a writer is an amateur does not afford any guarantee that what he has to say will be interesting. The memoirs of Doctor H—— would be wearisome from their mere monotonously moral note. And yet the man who wrote them, in his lowly environment, possessed an intellect quite out of the ordinary. This village doctor was philosopher as well as physician. Perhaps the closing pages of his journal might be

perused without any exceptional distaste. I venture
to transcribe them here :—

Extract from the Journal of the late Doctor H——,
Physician at Servigny (Aisne).

"It is an axiom of philosophy that nothing in
this world is either altogether bad or altogether
good. Pity, the tenderest, the most natural, the
most useful of the virtues, is not at all times in
place either with the soldier or the priest ; both
with priest and soldier there are occasions when
it must be held in restraint—when confronted by
the enemy, for instance. Officers do not make a
practice of recommending it on the eve of battle,
and in some old book I have read that Monsieur
Nicole held it in distrust as the motive principle
of concupiscence. There is nothing of the priest
about me, and still less of the soldier. I am a
doctor, and amongst the most insignificant of that
profession, a country doctor. I have practised
my art for long years and in obscurity, and I would
assert that if pity alone can be a worthy stimulus
to the adoption of our profession, we must lay it
aside finally when we encounter those miseries
which it has inspired us with the desire to alleviate.
A doctor whom pity accompanies to the bedside of
his patients will find his observation not sufficiently
acute, his hands not sufficiently steady. We go

wherever compassion for the human race calls, but we must leave pity behind us. Moreover, doctors for the most part find it an easy task to attain the callousness which is so necessary to them. That is a mental condition which cannot long elude them, and there are moral reasons for this. Pity speedily becomes blunted when brought into contact with suffering; there is less disposition to deplore those misfortunes for which alleviation can be procured; finally, to the physician an illness offers a succession of interesting phenomena.

"From the time when I began the practice of medicine I flung myself into it with ardour. In the bodily ills disclosed to me I saw only opportunities for the practical application of my art. When a complaint developed without complications, I was able to see beauty in its conformity to the normal type. Those phenomena of disease, which offered apparent anomalies, awakened curiosity in my mind; so that I was enamoured of disease. What am I saying? From the point of view I espoused disease and health were possessed of indisputable personality. As an enthusiastic observer of the human mechanism, I found as much to admire in its more baleful affections as in its most healthy compliance with law. Willingly should I have exclaimed with Pinel: 'What a magnificent cancer!' That was a fine attitude of

L

mind, and I was on my way to become a philosopher-physician. I only needed to have a genius for my art in order to enjoy completely, and enter into possession of, the full beauty of the theory of disease classification. It is the privilege of genius to unveil the splendour of things. Where the ordinary man would see only a disgusting wound, the naturalist worthy of the name stands enraptured before a battlefield on which the mysterious forces of life struggle for supremacy, in an encounter more inexorable, more terrifying than any that the strenuous abandon of Salvator Rosa ever depicted. I only caught glimpses of that spectacle of which the Magendies and Claude Bernards were familiar witnesses, and it was a distinction for me to do so ; but though resigned to the career of a humble practitioner, I fortified myself, as a professional duty, in the habit of confronting grievous situations unemotionally. I gave my patients my energies and my intellect. I did not give them pity. God forbid that I should place any gift, howsoever precious, above His gift of pity ! Pity is the widow's mite ; it is the incomparable offering of the poor man, who with generosity outstripping that of all the wealthy in this world of ours, gives with the gift of his tears a piece torn from his heart. For that very reason it is that pity must be dissociated from the carry-

ing out of a professional duty, how noble soe'er
that profession may be.

"To enter upon more particular considerations,
I would say that the folk in whose midst I am
living evoke in their misfortunes a sentiment
which is not pity.   There is something of truth in
the theory that a man cannot inspire in another
an emotion which he is incapable of experiencing
himself.   Now the peasantry in our part of the
country are not tender-hearted.   Harsh to others
as to themselves, they drag out an existence morose
in its gravity.   That gravity, too, is contagious,
and in their company sadness and dejection affect
one's mind.   What is fine about their moral out-
look is that they preserve unscathed the nobler
features of humanity.   As they are not accustomed
to think with any frequency or profundity, their
thoughts assume naturally in certain circumstances
a solemn tone.   I have heard some of them give
utterance at the point of death to brief, forcible
speeches worthy of the patriarchs of the Old
Testament.   They can call forth one's admiration,
but do not awaken one's sympathies.   With them
everything is quite simple, even their illnesses.
Their sufferings are not accentuated by their imagination.   They are not like those over-sensitive
creatures who construct from their ills a monster
more harassing than the ills themselves.   They

meet death so much as a matter of course that it is
impossible to be greatly disturbed. To sum up, I
might say that they are all so much alike that no
shred of individuality vanishes as each one passes
away.

" For the reasons which I have just set down it
follows that I practise my profession of village
doctor very peacefully. I never regret having
chosen it. I sometimes think I am a little above
it ; but if it is vexatious to a man to feel himself
above his position, the annoyance would certainly
be greater if he felt unequal to it. I am not rich,
and never shall be so long as I live. But of what
use would money be to one who leads a solitary
village life ? My little grey mare, Jenny, is as yet
only fifteen years old, and she still trots as easily as
in the days of her first youth, especially when we
are going in the direction of the stable. I do not,
like my illustrious fellow-physicians in Paris, possess
a gallery of pictures for the entertainment of my
visitors, but I can show pear trees which the towns-
men have nothing like. My orchard is famous for
twenty leagues round, and the owners of the neighbouring châteaux come to beg cuttings from me.

" Now on a certain Monday—it will be a year ago
this very day—as I was busy in my garden inspecting
my espaliers, a farm servant came to beg me to call
as soon as possible at Les Alies.

"I asked him whether Jean Blin, the farmer at Les Alies, had sustained a fall the previous day as he came home in the evening. For in my part of the country a sprain is a common Sunday occurrence, and it is not at all rare for a man to break two or three ribs that day on leaving the public-house. Jean Blin is not exactly a bad sort, but he likes drinking in company, and more than once he has known what it is like to wait for Monday's dawn at the bottom of a miry ditch.

"The farm servant replied that there was nothing the matter with Jean Blin, but that Éloi, Jean's little son, was seized with fever.

"Without another thought for my espaliers, I went in search of my hat and stick, and set out on foot for Les Alies, which is only twenty minutes' walk from my house. As I walked, my thoughts were on ahead with Jean Blin's little boy in the grip of a fever. His father was a peasant much like every other peasant, with this peculiar difference, that the Intelligence which created him forgot to provide him with a brain. This great hulking Jean Blin has a head as thick as his fist. Divine wisdom has only furnished that particular skull with what was strictly indispensable, there's no getting over that. His wife, the best-looking woman in the place, is a noisy, bustling housewife, stolidly virtuous. Well, well! To this worthy couple a child had been given, who was easily the most delicate, the most spiritual little being that ever adorned this old world of ours. Heredity is responsible for some of the surprises in nature, and it has been well said that nobody knows what he is about when he father's a child. Heredity, according to our honoured Nysten, is the biological phenomenon which is responsible for the fact that, in addition to the normal type of the species, ancestors transmit to their descendants certain peculiarities of organization and of aptitude. I admit it. But what peculiarities are transmitted and what are not, that is what is not very clear, even after a perusal of the learned works of Doctor Lucas and Monsieur Ribot. My neighbour, the notary, lent me last year a volume by Monsieur Émile Zola, and I observe that that author takes credit for particular discernment in this respect. 'Here,' he says, in substance, 'is an ancestor afflicted with neurosis; his descendants will show neuropathic tendencies, that is to say, when they do not do so; amongst them will be found some foolish and some intelligent individuals; one of them may even be a genius.' He has gone to the trouble of drawing up a genealogical chart to make his idea more easily apprehended. Well and good! The discovery is not particularly novel, and its expounder would unquestionably be ill-advised to vaunt himself upon it; it is none the less true, however, that it embraces practically all we know on the subject of heredity. And this is how it came about that Éloi, Jean Blin's little son, was an embodied intellect. He had the creative imagination. Many a time, when he was no higher than my walking-stick, I have come across him playing truant with the village urchins. Whilst they were reaching after nests, I have watched the little fellow constructing model mills and miniature syphons with pipes of straw. Inventive and unsociable he turned to nature. His schoolmaster despaired of ever making anything of so inattentive a child ; and, to tell the truth, at eight years old Éloi was still ignorant of his letters. But at that age he learned to read and write with astonishing rapidity, and in six months became the best scholar in the village.

"He was the most affectionate and the most clinging child. I gave him a few lessons in mathematics, and was astounded at the fertility that his mind displayed at this early age. In fact—I own it without any fear of being ridiculed, for in an old man cut off from civilization some exaggeration is pardonable—I rejoiced to have detected in this little peasant the premonitions of one of those enlightened spirits which at long intervals shine forth in the midst of our purblind race, and, impelled alike by the need of lavishing their affection and the desire for knowledge, are bound to effect something useful or beautiful wherever fate may assign them a place.

"My mind was occupied with musings of this kind as far as Les Alies. Entering the low-ceiled room, I found little Éloi ensconced in the big bed with cotton hangings, to which no doubt his parents had removed him on account of the gravity of his condition. He was lethargic; his head, though small and delicate, nevertheless made as great a dent in the pillow as if it had been of enormous weight. I stole near. His forehead was on fire; there was a disquieting redness about the conjunctive membrane; the temperature of the body was altogether too high. His mother and grandmother kept close to him, anxiously. Jean Blin, whose uneasiness prevented him from working, not knowing what to do, and being afraid to go away, stood with his hands in his pockets looking inquiringly first at one and then at another. The child turned his drawn face towards me, and scrutinizing me with an affectionate but heartbreaking glance, said in reply to my questions that his forehead and his eyes were both very painful, that he could hear noises which he knew were imaginary, and that he knew perfectly well who I was, his dear old friend.

"'First he has shivering fits, and then he is feverishly hot,' said his mother.

" Jean Blin, after ruminating for several minutes, remarked—

"' My belief is that what ails him is his inside.'

" Then he relapsed into silence.

" It had been only too easy for me to diagnose the symptoms of acute meningitis. I prescribed revulsive applications to the feet, and leeches behind the ears. I drew near to my little friend a second time, and tried to say something cheerful to him, more cheerful, alas ! than facts warranted. But I was suddenly aware of an entirely new personal experience. Although I was completely self-possessed I seemed to see the sick child through a veil, and at such a distance that he appeared quite, quite small. This upsetting of my ideas of space was speedily followed by an analogous upheaval of my ideas of time. Although my visit had not lasted above five minutes, I received the impression that I had been in that low-ceiled room, in front of that bed with its white cotton hangings, for a long time, for a very long time, and that months and even years had rolled by whilst I was held motionless.

" By a mental effort which is perfectly natural to me, I there and then put these singular impressions under analysis, and the cause of them became quite clear to me. It was simple enough. Éloi was dear to me. At the sight of him so unexpectedly and so seriously ill I could not 'get my bearings.'

It is the popular phrase, and it is appropriate. Moments of anguish appear to us unnaturally long. That is why I received the impression that the five or six minutes I had passed beside Éloi had something interminable about them. As to the fancy that the child was at a distance from me, that came from the idea that I was about to lose him. This idea, impressed on me against my will, had from the first moment assumed a character of absolute certainty.

"The following day Éloi was in a less alarming condition. The improvement continued for several days. I had sent into the town to procure ice, and this had had a good effect. But on the fifth day I recognized that he was in violent delirium. He talked a great deal, and amongst the disconnected words I heard him pouring out I could distinguish these—

"'The balloon! the balloon! I have hold of the helm of the balloon. It rises. The sky is inky. Mamma, mamma! why won't you come with me? I am steering my balloon to a place where it will be so beautiful! Come, it is stifling here.'

"That day Jean Blin followed me up the road. He slouched along with that air of embarrassment a man has who wants to say something and is yet afraid to say it. At last, after walking some twenty paces with me in silence, he stopped, and laying his hand on my arm said—

" ' See here, Doctor, it's my belief that what ails the little chap is his inside.'

" I continued my way sorrowfully, and for the first time in my life my eagerness to see once more my pears and apricots did not avail to mend my pace. For the first time in forty years of practice I found the plight of one of my patients heart-rending, and in my inmost self I bewailed the child I was powerless to save.

" Distracting pangs soon came to magnify my grief. I feared that my treatment had contributed to the development of the disease. I caught myself forgetting in the morning what I had prescribed the night before, uncertain in my diagnosis, nervous, and worried. I called in one of my fellow-practitioners, a clever young fellow, who had a practice in the next village. When he arrived, the poor little fellow, whose sight was already gone, was plunged in a profound coma.

" The following day he died.

" A year having elapsed after this misfortune, it happened that I was called in consultation to the county town. The fact is singular. The causes which led up to it are extraordinary ; but as they have no connection with what I am relating, I do not record them here. After the consultation, Dr.

C——, physician to the prefecture, did me the
honour to invite me to lunch with him and two
other members of the profession. After lunch,
where I found refreshment in conversation at once
erudite and diversified, coffee was served to us in
the doctor's sanctum. As I approached the mantelpiece to put down my empty cup, I saw hanging
upon the mirror-frame a portrait which aroused in
me so profound an emotion that it was with difficulty I refrained from crying out. It was a miniature, the portrait of a child. This child resembled
in so striking a fashion the one I had been unable
to cure—the child of whom I had been constantly
thinking for a year past—that for a moment I could
not avoid the thought that it was he himself. That
supposition, however, was of course absurd. The
black wooden frame, with the circlet of gold surrounding the miniature, proclaimed the taste of the
end of the eighteenth century, and the child was
depicted in a vest of pink and white striped material such as the little Louis XVII might have worn ;
but the face was out-and-out the face of my little
Éloi. The same forehead, imperious and powerful
—the forehead of a man beneath the curls of a
cherub ; the same fire in the eyes, the same suffering grace on the lips ! Indeed, to the very same
features was joined the identical expression !

" I had probably been examining this portrait for

quite a long while when Dr. C——, clapping me on the shoulder, said—

"'Ah, my friend, you have before you a family relic which I am proud to possess. My maternal grandfather was the friend of the illustrious man whom you see painted there in the days of his early boyhood, and it was from my grandfather that that miniature came into my possession.'

"I asked him to be good enough to tell me the name of his grandfather's illustrious friend. Upon this he unhooked the miniature and held it out to me:

"'See,' he said, 'on the exergue . . . *Lyon,* 1787. Doesn't that recall anything to you? No? Well, that child of twelve was the great Ampère.'

"Then, in a flash, I had an exact perception, an unequivocal estimate of what death had swept away one year previously in the farmhouse of Les Alies."

MEMOIRS OF A VOLUNTEER

TO PAUL ARENE

MEMOIRS OF A VOLUNTEER[1]

I

I WAS born in seventeen hundred and seventy in the rural outskirts of a small town in the Langres district, where my father, half townsman and half peasant, dealt in cutlery and tended his orchards. In this place certain nuns, although they only educated girls, consented to teach me to read since I was but a child, and they were good friends of my mother. On leaving their hands I took lessons in Latin from a priest in the town, a shoemaker's son, well grounded in the humanities. In the summer the shade of some old chestnut-trees served as a schoolroom, and close beside his hives the Abbé Lamadou interpreted Virgil's *Georgics* to me. I never dreamed that any one could be happier than I, and between my master and Mlle. Rose, the marshal's daughter,

[1] All the incidents in these memoirs are authentic, and may be traced to various documents of the eighteenth century. Not a single detail, however apparently insignificant, is made use of for which indubitable authority cannot be produced. (AUTHOR.)

I lived in great contentment. But in this world no
happiness is enduring. One morning, as my mother
embraced me, she slipped an écu of six livres into
my coat pocket. My luggage was packed. My father
leaped on his horse and, taking me up behind him,
carried me off to the college at Langres. All the
time the journey lasted I was dreaming of my own
little room, scented towards autumn time with the
perfume of the fruit stored up in the loft; or of
the close where my father took me on Sunday to
gather apples from the trees he had grafted with
his own hand; of Rose, of my sisters, of my
mother; even of myself, unhappy exile! I could
feel my heart thump, and it was with difficulty that
I held back the tears which filled my eyelids. At
length, after five hours' journey, we reached the
town and set foot to ground in front of a huge
door, on which I read with a shudder the word
College. The principal, Father Féval, of the Oratory,
received us in a big saloon with whitewashed walls.
He was still a young man, of impressive appearance,
and I found his smile reassuring. On all such
occasions my father had displayed a naturalness,
vivacity, and candour which never deserted him.

"Reverend Father," he said, placing his hand
on me, "I bring you here my only son. His name is
Pierre, after his godfather, and Aubier, his father's
name, which I have handed on to him as stainless

as I received it from my late dear father. Pierre is my only boy ; his mother, Madeleine Ordalu, having presented me with one son and three daughters, whom I am bringing up to the best of my ability. To my daughters will fall the lot which it shall please God in the first place, and later on their husbands, to assign to them. They are said to be pretty, and I can't help believing it myself. But beauty is only a gay deceiver which it is best not to take into account. They will be handsome enough if they are only good enough. As to my son Pierre here before you (as he pronounced these words my father put his hand so heavily on my shoulder that he made me flinch), provided that he fears God and knows enough Latin, he is to be a priest. Very humbly then, reverend father, I beg you to examine him at your leisure, so as to ascertain his genuine capacities. If you find any merit in him, let him remain with you. I will willingly pay whatever is needful. If, on the contrary, you consider that you can make nothing of him, send me word, and I will come and fetch him away at once, and teach him how to make knives like his father. For I am a cutler, at your service, reverend sir."

Father Féval agreed to undertake what was asked of him. And upon this assurance, my father took leave of the principal and of me also. As he was very moved, and had some trouble to restrain his sobs, he assumed a stiff and harsh expression, and under the semblance of a farewell embrace bestowed a terrific thump. When he was gone, Father Féval drew me away from the parlour into a garden surrounded by a thick hedge. Then, as we passed beneath the shade of the trees, he said to me—

"O Sylvaï dulces umbras frondosaï!"[1]

I was fortunate enough to recognize in these archaic inflexions and ponderous prosody a line from old Ennius, and I replied glibly to Father Féval that Virgil was even more worthy than his antique predecessor to celebrate the beauty of these cool shades, *frigus opacum*. The principal seemed quite gratified at this compliment. He questioned me benevolently upon some rudimentary points, and when he had heard my replies—

"That will do," he said. "If you work hard, very hard indeed, you will be able to keep up with the fourth class. Come with me. I should like to introduce you myself to your master and your fellow-pupils."

Whilst our little walk lasted, my forlornness had somewhat abated, and I was conscious of feeling supported in my distress. But no sooner did I

---

[1] O leafy woods diffusing grateful shade!

find myself surrounded by my class-fellows and in the presence of Monsieur Joursanvault, my master, than I sank back into abject despair. Monsieur Joursanvault was neither easy of access nor the possessor of the principal's fine simplicity. He appeared to me very much more impressed with his own importance, and also more harsh and reserved. He was a little man with a big head, and his words found egress with a whistling noise between two white lips and four yellow teeth. I decided immediately that such a mouth as his was never intended to pronounce the name Lavinia, a name which I loved even better than that of Rose. For I may as well own it, the idyllic and royal fiancée of the unfortunate Turnus had been decked by my imagination with the most august charms. The ideal image I had formed of her sufficed to eclipse the more everyday beauty of the marshal's daughter. Monsieur Joursanvault then, the master of the fourth class, pleased me little enough. My class-fellows inspired me with fear : they had every appearance of being unspeakably venturesome, and it was not without reason that I dreaded that my simplicity might goad them to ridicule. I was very much inclined to cry.

Self-respect, a more powerful emotion than my grief, alone enabled me to restrain my tears.

When evening came, I left the college and went

off into the town in search of the quarters which my father had bespoken for me. I was to lodge with five other scholars at the house of an artisan, whose wife would do our cooking. Every month each of us paid him twenty-five sous.

At the outset my schoolfellows tried to tease me about my ill-cut clothes and my rustic appearance, but they gave up their efforts when they saw that they did not vex me. One of their number alone, the consumptive son of a lawyer, continued insolently to imitate my lumpish, awkward carriage, but I punished him with a fist so unexpectedly weighty that he was not disposed to resume his performance. Monsieur Joursanvault did not take very kindly to me, but as I fulfilled my tasks with regularity, I provided him with no occasion for punishment. As he displayed his authority in a violent, uncertain, and irritating fashion, he invited rebellion, and, as a matter of fact, there were several mutinous episodes in his class in which I, however, took no part. One day, as I was walking in the garden with the principal, who showed himself very kindly disposed to me, unluckily it came into my head to boast to him of my good conduct.

"Father," said I, "I took no part in the last escapade."

"There's nothing to boast about in that," replied Father Féval, with a touch of contempt which rent my heart.

He hated meanness above everything in the world. I made up my mind as he spoke never again to say or do anything despicable. And if from that day forward I have managed to keep free from lying and mean-spiritedness, I owe it entirely to that excellent man.

Monsieur Féval was in no respect a philosopher-priest; he exercised the virtues, but not the doctrines, of Rousseau's Vicaire Savoyard. He believed everything a priest ought to believe. But he had a horror of mummery, and could not endure the idea of demanding the interposition of God in trifling affairs. This appeared clearly enough on the Christmas Day when Monsieur Joursanvault came to him with a complaint against the impious jesters who, on the eve of the festival, had put ink in the holy water stoups.

The scandalized Joursanvault mumbled anathemas, and murmured—

"There is no disputing the fact, it is a black deed!"

"By reason of the ink," replied our good principal calmly.

That upright man regarded weakness as the direct source of all ills. He often said: "Lucifer and the rebellious angels erred through pride. It is on that account that even in hell they have not ceased to hold rank as princes and kings, and to maintain an awful supremacy over the souls of the damned. If they had fallen through pettiness, in the midst of the flames they would now be the laughing-stock and sport of sinners, and the empery of evil would have slipped from their dishonoured hands."

When the holidays came round it was a great joy to me to see my home once more. But I found it unaccountably shrunken. As I entered, my mother, bending over the hearth, was skimming the soup-kettle. She, too, my dear mother, seemed strangely diminutive to me, and I sobbed as I flung my arms round her.

With the skimmer in her hand she told me how age and trouble had rendered my father inactive, so that he was no longer able to look after his orchard; how my eldest sister was promised in marriage to the cooper's son; how the sacristan of the parish had been found dead in his chamber, with a bottle in his hand, which his stark fingers clutched so firmly by the neck that it was thought at first that it could never be loosened from his hold. Yet it was scarcely decent to bear the sacristan's body to the church still grasping his bottle of wish-wash. As I listened to my mother a clear realization of the flight of time and the passing of things temporal for the first time reached my brain. I fell into a sort of reverie.

"Well, well, my boy," said my mother, "you look flourishing. Why, with your dimity jacket, you are already the very spit of a little *curé*."

At this moment Mademoiselle Rose came into the room, blushing and feigning to be completely surprised at the sight of me. I saw that she was interested in me, and felt secretly flattered. But in her presence I assumed the grave and reserved demeanour of the ecclesiastic. The greater part of these holidays I spent in walks with Monsieur Lamadou.

It had been agreed between us that we should talk nothing but Latin. So we went our ways through the midst of the lowly tasks of the tillers of the soil, with nature riotous around us, side by side, straight before us, grave, serious, guileless, disdainful of such utterly vain and common pleasures as we had knowledge of.

I returned to the college with the firm determination to take Holy Orders. Already I could see myself, like Monsieur Lamadou, wearing a great three-cornered hat and a cassock, with black breeches, woollen stockings, and buckled shoes, occupied now with the eloquence of Cicero, now with the doctrine of St. Augustine, and gravely acknowledging the salutes of the women and the

poor folk who bowed to me as I threaded
my way through the crowd. Alas! a woman's
shadow began to disturb this peaceful dream. Up
to that time I had known nothing of women, except
Lavinia in the *Æneid* and Mademoiselle Rose.
Then I realized Dido, and flames seemed to rush
through my veins. The image of the unhappy
Queen, who, tortured by an irremediable wound,
wandered in the forest of myrtles, bent at night
over my troubled couch.

Moreover, if I walked out in the evening, I
seemed to be aware of her dead white figure glid-
ing between the bushes in the woods as the moon
passes through the midst of the clouds. Obsessed
by this dazzling image, I began to waver about
taking Orders. Nevertheless, I assumed the dress
of the ecclesiastic, which suited me admirably.
When I visited my home for the first time thus
attired, my mother curtsied to me, and Rose hid
her face in her apron and wept. Then turning on
me her lovely eyes, as pellucid as her tears, she
said—

"I can't think what I am crying about, Monsieur
Pierre!"

In this mood she was touching. But she did not
in the least resemble the moon seen through the
clouds. I did not love her; it was Dido I loved.

That year was signalized to me by a dreadful

calamity. I lost my father, who sank very suddenly under an attack of water on the chest.

In his last moments he adjured his children to live honestly and piously, and blessed them. He died with a degree of resignation which was not in the least consonant with his character. It appeared to be without regret, with cheerfulness even, that he quitted a life to which he was strongly attached by all the bonds of a nature essentially vivacious. From him I learnt that it is easier to die than one would think, if one is but a good man.

I resolved that I, in my turn, would act a father's part to those elder sisters already marriageable, and to that tearful mother who, year by year, seemed to grow smaller, weaker, and more appealing.

Thus, then, in one moment, from a child I became a man. I finished my studies at the Oratory under excellent masters—Fathers Lance, Porriquet, and Marion, who had buried themselves in a wild and remote province to devote their brilliant faculties and a profound erudition which would have done honour to the Academy of Inscriptions to the education of a few poor children. The principal surpassed them all in loftiness of intellect and beauty of soul.

Whilst I was finishing my philosophical studies under those eminent teachers, a widespread rumour was conveyed to our distant province, and even penetrated the cloistral walls of the college. There was gossip about a convocation of the States General, and reforms were clamoured for, and great changes expected. Some of the new publications which our masters permitted us to read proclaimed the approaching return of the Golden Age.

When the moment came for me to leave the college, I wept as I embraced Father Féval.

He held me clasped in his arms with profound emotion. Then he led me to the hedge-sheltered path where six years previously I had had my first conversation with him.

There, taking me by the hand, he bent over me, and looked into my eyes and said—

"Remember, dear child, that without principle intellect goes for nothing. You will perhaps live long enough to see the dawn of a new régime in this land of ours. These great changes cannot be brought about without disturbances. May you bear in mind in the midst of them what I am telling you now : in difficult situations intellect is but a sorry shield : virtue alone can suffice to safeguard him who merits safety."

Whilst he discoursed in this vein we emerged from the arbour, and the sun, already low on the horizon, bathed him in its warm crimson rays and lit up his handsome, thoughtful countenance. I was fortunate enough to retain a vivid impression of his words, which struck me forcibly, although at the time they were a little above my head. At that date I was only a schoolboy, and not a very brilliant one. Since then my eyes have been opened to the profundity and truth of his maxims by the terrible object-lesson of subsequent events.

II

HAD abandoned the idea of taking Orders. It was necessary to earn a livelihood. I had not learnt Latin with the idea of making cutlery in the suburbs of a small town. I indulged in ambitious dreams. Our little holding, our cows, our garden, were far from equal to the fulfilment of my ambitions. I discovered rusticity in Mademoiselle Rose. My mother conceived that a town such as Paris was necessary to the full development of my abilities. Without much difficulty I myself came to a similar conclusion. I ordered a coat from the best tailor in Langres. With this coat went a steel-hilted sword, which threw back the skirts and invested one with so smart an air that I doubted nothing I was on the road to fortune. Father Féval gave me a letter of recommendation to the Duc de Puybonne, and on the 12th of July, in the year of grace 1789, I climbed into the coach, not without tears, laden with Latin books, cakes, bacon, and kisses. I entered Paris by the Faubourg St.

Antoine, which appeared to me more hideous than the most squalid hamlets in my own province. With all my heart I bewailed both the unhappy folk who had their dwelling there and myself who had forsaken my father's house and orchard land to seek advancement amidst such a tatterdemalion crew. A wine merchant who had been my fellow-traveller explained, however, that these people were all in ecstasies over the destruction of an old prison known as the Bastille-St.-Antoine. He assured me that Monsieur Necker would soon bring back the Golden Age. But a wigmaker, who overheard our conversation, declared that, on the contrary, unless the King speedily dismissed him, Monsieur Necker would ruin the country.

"The Revolution," he added, "is a terrible misfortune. Nobody now dresses his hair. And people who neglect that duty are below the level of the beasts."

These words angered the wine merchant.

"Know, master barber," he interposed, "that a rejuvenescent race disdains idle trappings. I would punish you for your impertinence, if I had time to do so ; but I am on my way to supply wine to Monsieur Bailly, the Mayor of Paris, who honours me with his friendship."

In this fashion they parted ; and as for me, I betook myself on foot, with my Latin books, my bacon, and the memory of my mother's kisses to the house of the Duc de Puybonne, to present my letter of recommendation. His mansion was situated at the other end of the city in the Rue de Grenelle. The passers-by vied with one another in supplying me with directions, for the Duke was celebrated for his benevolence.

He received me cordially. Everything in his dress and in his manners was of the utmost simplicity. He had that contented demeanour which one only meets with in men who labour assiduously without being compelled.

He read Father Féval's letter, and remarked—

"This is a satisfactory letter of recommendation, but what are your acquirements ?"

I replied that I was acquainted with Latin, a little Greek, ancient history, rhetoric, and poetry.

"What a list of accomplishments ! " he rejoined, smiling. "But it would have been more to the point if you had had some notion of agriculture, the mechanical arts, commerce, banking, and industry. You are acquainted with the laws of Solon, now, I'll wager ?"

I signified that I was.

"Very good, very good. But you know nothing about the English constitution. But no matter. You are young, and of an age to acquire knowledge. I will give you a place about my person, with an allowance of five hundred écus. Monsieur Mille, my secretary, will instruct you as to the duties I shall expect you to perform. Au revoir, monsieur."

A lackey conducted me to Monsieur Mille, who was writing at a table in the middle of a spacious white apartment. He signalled to me to wait. He was a little roundabout man, and his appearance was pleasant, but he rolled his eyes about ferociously, and seemed to be scolding under his breath as he wrote.

I heard him give utterance to the following words: "Tyrants, fetters, hell, man, Rome, slavery, liberty."[1] I concluded he was mad. But when he had laid his pen aside he nodded his head to me and smiled.

"Well?" he said. "You are examining the apartment. It is as severe as that of an ancient Roman. No gilding on the panels, no fal-lals on the mantelpiece; nothing is left to remind us of the detestable times of the late king, nothing remains that is derogatory to the dignity of a free man (*un homme libre*). *Libre, Tibre.* I must jot that rhyme down. It's a good one, now, isn't it? Are you fond of verse, Monsieur Pierre Aubier?"

I replied that I was only too much devoted to it,

---

[1] "*Tyrans, fers, enfers, homme, Rome, esclavage, liberté.*" Monsieur Mille is, of course, engaged in a search for rhymes. (TRANS.)

N

and that it would have served me better when I presented myself before the Duke if I had preferred Mr. Burke to Virgil.

"Virgil is a great man," replied Monsieur Mille. "But what is your opinion of Monsieur Chénier? For my part I know nothing finer than his *Charles IX*. I will not attempt to conceal from you that I am myself experimenting in tragedy, and at the very moment you entered I was finishing a scene with which I am not a little pleased. You appear to me to be a very trustworthy person. I am quite willing to confide in you so far as to tell you what my tragedy is about, but you mustn't breathe a word. You realize how far-reaching the least indiscretion might be. I am composing a tragedy upon the subject of Lucretia."

Then taking up a large manuscript book he read out: "*Lucretia, a tragedy in five acts, dedicated to Louis the Well Beloved, the restorer of liberty to France.*"

He spouted some two hundred lines to me and then broke off, saying in excuse that the remainder was as yet uncorrected.

"The Duke's post-bag," he said with a sigh, "robs me of the best hours of the day. We are in correspondence with all the enlightened men in England, Switzerland, and America. And talking of this, I may tell you, Monsieur Aubier, that your employment will consist of copying and classifying letters. If you would like to be informed without delay as to the matters which are occupying our attention at this very moment, I will tell you. At Puybonne we are superintending a farm where certain English experts have been engaged to introduce into France such agricultural improvements as have been attained in Great Britain. We are importing from Spain a number of those silky-fleeced sheep the flocks of which have enriched Segovia with their wool. This is so arduous an undertaking that we have been compelled to enlist the co-operation of the King himself. Lastly, we are buying cows in Switzerland to present to our dependents.

"I can say nothing on the subject of our correspondence upon public affairs. Entire secrecy is preserved as to that. But you are, of course, aware that the efforts of the Duc de Puybonne are directed towards the introduction into France of the English constitutional system. Pardon my leaving you, Monsieur Aubier. I am due at the Comédie Française. *Alzire* is to be performed."

That night I slept in fine linen sheets, and I did not sleep well. I dreamed that my mother's bees were flying over the ruins of the Bastille and around the Duc de Puybonne, who smiled graciously, and was enveloped in an unearthly radiance.

The following morning at an early hour I betook myself to Monsieur Mille's room, and asked him if he had enjoyed himself at the theatre.   He replied that he ventured to believe that the performance of *Alzire* had given him a clue to some of the methods by which Monsieur de Voltaire stirred the emotions of his audience.   Then he set me to work copying letters referring to the purchase of the Swiss cows, which the generous magnate was bestowing on his dependents.   Whilst I occupied myself with this task, Monsieur Mille said to me—

"The Duke is kind-hearted.   I have recorded his benevolent disposition in certain verses with which I am not ill-pleased.   Are you acquainted with the Puybonne estate?   No!   It is a domain of enchantment.   My lines may open your eyes to its charms.   I will recite them to you—

> Delightful valley, haven of repose,
> Groves ever verdant, where the limpid stream
> Peacefully onward flows,
> Whose dulcet murmurings seem
> Like note of birds, chanting their amorous woes;
> How my heart thrills your rural charms to view,
> And longings seize me, 'neath your sheltering boughs
> Her cherished name i' the beech's bark to hew.
> In this fair spot our Puybonne reigns,
> And uprightness and charity
> Silently bear him company,
> His spirit our happiness sustains.

> The frolic shepherds, at his call,
> Under the elms together come,
> Who to his bounty, one and all,
> Owe flocks, and herds, and home."[1]

I was astounded. At Langres I had never heard anything so courtly, and I was impressed with the fact that the air of Paris contained a something inexpressible, which it was useless to seek elsewhere.

After dinner I set out to inspect the principal edifices of the town. The genius of art has spent two centuries in distributing his treasures on the glorious banks of the Seine. Hitherto I had only been acquainted with Gothic castles and churches, and their melancholy character, tinged with un-

---

[1] Vallon délicieux, asile du repos,
Bocages toujours verts, où l'onde la plus pure
    Roule paisiblement ses flots,
    Et vient mêler son doux murmure
    Aux tendres concerts des oiseaux,
Que mon cœur est ému de vos beautés champêtres !
Que j'aime à confier, sous ces riants berceaux,
Le doux nom d'une nymphe à l'écorce des hêtres.
    De ces beaux lieux Puybonne est possesseur ;
Avec lui la bonté, la douce bienfaisance,
Dans ce palais habite en silence :
Le sentiment y retient le bonheur.
Puybonne enseigne aux folâtres bergères
    A s'assembler sous les ormeaux,
Il se mêle parfois à leurs danses légères,
Puis il leur donne des troupeaux.

couthness, only awakens displeasing thoughts in the mind. Paris, it is true, still contains a certain number of these barbaric structures. The cathedral itself, which rises in that quarter of the town to which the term City is specially assigned, bears witness by the irregularity and confusion of its plan to the ignorance of the age in which it was erected. Parisians overlook its hideousness on the score of its antiquity. Father Féval was accustomed to say that everything antique is worthy of respect.

But what a different aspect do the buildings of the more cultured ages present! A regularity in plan, an exact proportion between the component parts, an uncrowded arrangement in the grouping, and then the charm of the various orders copied from the antique—all these qualities dazzle one in the creations of modern architects, and all unite to render the colonnade of the Louvre a masterpiece worthy of France and its kings. Ah, what a town is Paris! Monsieur Mille showed me the theatre where the finest actresses in the world ally their voices and their charms to the inspired compositions of Mozart and Gluck. And in addition, he even took me to the gardens of the Luxembourg, where beneath the shade of venerable trees I saw Raynal walking side by side with Dussaulx. Ah, my honoured principal, my master, my father, my beloved Monsieur Féval! Would that you were witness to the joy, the rapture of your pupil, your son!

For six weeks I led the pleasantest of lives. All around me I heard talk of the return of the Golden Age, and I began to believe in the approach of the car bearing Saturn and Rhea within it. In the mornings, under Monsieur Mille's direction, I made copies of letters.

Monsieur Mille was a boon companion, always smiling, always uttering flowery speeches, always volatile as a zephyr.

After dinner I would read a few pages of the Encyclopædia to our worthy employer, and then I was free till the following morning. One night I went with Monsieur Mille to supper at the Porcherons. At the entrance of this place of amusement stood a group of women wearing the national colours in their caps, and carrying flowers in a basket. One of them, approaching me, took me by the arm and said, " See, little master, I make you a present of this bunch of roses."

I blushed, and was at a loss what to say in reply. But Monsieur Mille, who knew the ways of the town, said to me—

" You must give a six-sous piece in exchange for those roses, and say something gallant to the pretty maiden."

I did both one and the other, and then inquired
of Monsieur Mille if he thought the flower-seller
was a well-conducted girl. He replied that there
was very little likelihood of it, but that it was a duty
to show courtesy to all women. Day by day I
became more attached to the excellent Duc de
Puybonne. He was the best and the most childlike
of men. He did not consider that he had given anything whatever to the unfortunate unless it had cost
him some self-sacrifice. He lived like a man of the
people, and regarded the luxury of the rich as a
preying upon the poor. His benefactions were well
considered. One day, addressing us both, he
said—

"No pleasure is more gratifying than to labour
for the happiness of people unknown to you,
whether by planting some useful tree, or by grafting
on young saplings in the woods buds from which
one day may spring fruit to assuage the thirst of
some traveller astray."

The worthy Duke found no interests except in
works of philanthropy. He laboured ardently to
secure new constitutional forms to the kingdom.
As a representative peer in the National Assembly
he took his seat in the ranks of those admirers of
English liberty who were styled monarchical, by
the side of Malouet and Stanislas de Clermont-Ton-
nerre. And although his party appeared even then

defeated, he awaited with all the fervour of indomitable hope the oncoming of revolution in its most humane aspect. We shared his aspirations.

Despite numerous causes for uneasiness, we continued during the following year to be upheld by this enthusiasm. I accompanied Monsieur Mille to the Champ de Mars at the beginning of July. On this spot two hundred thousand persons of all ranks—men, women, children—were erecting with their own hands the altar upon which all were to swear that they would live free, or, if needs must, die free. Wig-makers in blue jackets, water-carriers, abbés, coal-heavers, capuchins, opera-singers in brocaded dresses with ribbons and feathers in their hair, all these side by side delved the sacred soil of their country. What an object-lesson in fraternity ! We saw Monsieur Sieyès and Monsieur de Beauharnais trundling the same cart ; we saw Father Gérard, passing like an ancient Roman from the Senate to the plough, wielding the spade and preparing the ground ; we saw an entire family at work in the same spot—the father digging, the mother filling the wheelbarrow, and the children pushing it turn and turn about, whilst the youngest, only four years of age, borne in the arms of his grandfather aged ninety-three, lisped out : " *Ah ! ça ira ! ça ira !* " We saw the Society of Journeymen Gardeners marching in procession with lettuces

and daisies attached to the ends of their spades.
Several other corporations followed them, preceded
by a band : the Printers, whose banner bore this
inscription : *Printing, foremost ensign of Liberty*. Then
the Butchers : upon their standard was painted a
large knife, with these words : *Tremble, aristocrats !
Behold the Journeymen Butchers*.

And even this took on the appearance for us of
fraternity.

"Aubier, my friend, my brother," exclaimed Monsieur Mille, "I am fired with poetical enthusiasm.
I am about to compose an ode which shall be dedicated to you.   Listen :—

> Friend, behold the concourse grand,
>   From far and wide assembled there,
> The mainstays of our own loved land,
>   Whose banners proudly take the air :
> Love it is directs their path
>   Toward the patriot altar-fires,
> Each his bounden service hath
>   Vowed, till Life's last flame expires."[1]

---

[1] Ami, vois tu ce peuple immense,
   Comme il accourt de toutes parts :
   Des artisans chers à la France
   Vois-tu flotter les étendards ?
   C'est à l'autel de la Patrie.
   Que l'amour dirige leurs pas ;
   Tous vont à leur mère chérie
   Se dévouer jusqu'au trépas,

Monsieur Mille recited these lines heroically; he was little, but his gestures were magnificent. He was wearing an amaranth-coloured coat. These circumstances combined to draw attention to him, and by the time he had finished the foregoing he was surrounded by a ring of inquisitive people. He was applauded. In ecstasies, he went on—

> "Unseal your eyes, direct your minds
> Upon this solemn spectacle . . ." [1]

But scarcely had he uttered these words before a lady, decked with an immense black hat and feathers, flung herself into his arms and clasped him close against the fichu she wore round her shoulders.

"Ah, how splendid!" she cried. "Monsieur Mille, permit me to embrace you."

A Capuchin who occupied a place in the ring of onlookers, bent his chin down on to his spade and clapped his hands at the sight of such a capacious embrace. Then some of the young patriots who stood by pushed him laughingly in the direction of the demonstrative lady, who transferred her embraces to him in the midst of popular acclamations. Monsieur Mille embraced me, and I embraced Monsieur Mille.

"Such splendid lines!" cried the lady with the

---

[1] Ouvre tes yeux, fixe ton âme
Sur ce spectacle solennel . . .

outrageous hat. "Bravo, Mille! They are worthy of Jean Baptiste."

"Oh!" said Monsieur Mille, bashfully hanging his head, his cheeks round and red as apples.

"Yes, absolutely worthy of Jean Baptiste," repeated Madame. "They must be set to the tune of '*Le serin qui te fait envie*.'"[1]

"You are too flattering," Monsieur Mille replied. "Permit me, Madame Berthemet, to present to you my friend Pierre Aubier, a Limousin gentleman. He is a man of parts, and will soon be accustomed to the ways of Paris."

"The dear creature," Madame Berthemet rejoined, as she pressed my hand. "Let him come to see us. You must bring him, Monsieur Mille. We have a little music always on Thursdays. Is he fond of music? But what a foolish question! Only a barbarian given over to every savage passion could fail to love music. Come this next Thursday, Monsieur Aubier; my daughter Amélie will sing you a ballad."

As she spoke, Madame Berthemet motioned to a young lady dressed in white, with a Greek headdress, whose fair hair and blue eyes seemed to me the loveliest in the world. I blushed as I bowed. But she did not appear to notice my embarrassment.

[1] The canary which spurs you to rivalry.

As we returned to the Puybonne mansion I did not attempt to conceal from Monsieur Mille the profound impression the beauty of this charming creature had made on me.

"In that case," replied Monsieur Mille, "I shall have to add a strophe to my ode."

And after reflecting for a few seconds, he added, "There now, I have managed it.

> If some maiden, fair and fond,
>   To your wooing yields consent,
> Only wedlock's sacred bond
>   Must your mutual vows cement.
> But the altar where you hie
>   Must a patriot altar be,
> Or the Heaven you dare defy
>   Will avenge your treachery."[1]

Alas ! Monsieur Mille did not possess that gift of foretelling future events which was in former ages ascribed to poets. Our days of happiness were already numbered, and all our dazzling illusions were doomed to extinction. The day follow-

---

[1] Si d'une belle honnête et sage
>   Tu sais un jour te faire aimer,
> Le nœud sacré du mariage
>   Est le seul que tu dois former ;
> Mais à l'autel de la Patrie
>   Courez tous deux pour vous unir,
> Que jamais votre foi trahie
>   N'ordonne au ciel de vous punir.

ing the Federation fête the nation awakened to a sense of harrowing dissension. Weak and narrow-minded, the king ill fulfilled the limitless trust the people had placed in him.

The criminal emigration of princes and nobility was impoverishing the country, antagonizing the people, and conducing to war. The political clubs overawed the National Assembly. The acrimony of the populace became more and more menacing. And whilst the nation was a prey to agitators, neither did I possess my heart in peace. I had met Amélie again. I had become the constant guest of her family, and never a week passed that did not find me two or three times a visitor at the house they lived in, in the Rue Neuve St. Eustache. Their fortunes, at one time flourishing, had flagged considerably owing to the Revolution, and I may venture to say that ill-luck ripened our friendship. As Amélie became poorer I found myself more sympathetic, and I loved her. I loved without hope. Who was I, poor little peasant lad, that I should be pleasing to so charming a townswoman?

I marvelled at her gifts. By composing music, painting, or translating some English romance, she courageously shut out the consciousness of misfortune, both public and private. Whenever she saw any one she displayed an aloofness which, so far as I was concerned, would relapse freely into playful banter. It was clear that though her heart was untouched she found my company diverting. Her father was the handsomest grenadier in the district, but in all other respects a nonentity. As to Madame Berthemet, she was, despite a petulant disposition, the best of women. She was brimming with enthusiasm. She appreciated parakeets, political economists, and Monsieur Mille's poetry to the swooning point. She was fond of me when she could spare time, but much of hers was taken up by the gazettes and the opera. Next to her daughter there was no one in the world whom it gave me greater pleasure to meet.

I had progressed greatly in the good graces of the Duc de Puybonne. I was no longer engaged in the copying of letters : he entrusted me with the most delicate transactions, and often confided to me matters as to which Monsieur Mille himself was left in ignorance.

Moreover, he had lost faith, if not courage. The humiliating flight of Louis XVI distressed him more than I can say; yet after the return from Varennes he appeared unintermittently in the entourage of the royal prisoner, who had despised his advice and been suspicious of his loyalty. My dear master remained immutably faithful to moribund royalty. On the 10th of August he was at the Château, and it was by a sort of miracle that he

eluded the mob and managed to get back to his
house. During the night I was summoned to him.
I found him disguised in the clothes of one of his
stewards.

"Farewell," he said to me. "I am leaving a
country delivered over to all sorts of abominations
and crimes. The day after to-morrow I shall have
landed on the coast of England. I am taking with
me three hundred louis ; it is all I have been able
to get together of what I own. I am leaving behind me property to a considerable amount. I
have no one to trust my interests to but yourself. Mille is a fool. Take my affairs into your
keeping. I know that you will incur danger in
doing so ; but I think highly enough of you to
burden you with a compromising load."

I seized his hands, kissed them, and bathed them
with tears ; it was my only answer.

Whilst he escaped from Paris under cover of
his disguise and a forged passport with which he
was provided, I burned in the various fireplaces in
the house papers which would have sufficed to
compromise whole families, and cost the lives of
hundreds of people. During the days that followed
I was lucky enough to be able to dispose—at very
poor prices, it is true—of the Duc de Puybonne's
carriages, horses, and plate, and in this fashion I
salvaged some seventy or eighty thousand livres,

which crossed the Channel. It was not without encountering the greatest dangers that I carried these delicate negotiations through. My life hung in the balance. The Terror prevailed in the capital the day following the 10th of August. In those streets which only the previous evening were enlivened by the motley variety of costumes, where the cries of hawkers and the clatter of horses had resounded, solitude and silence now reigned. All the shops were closed ; the citizens, concealed in their dwellings, trembled both for their friends and for themselves.

The barriers were guarded, and it was impossible for any one to leave the appalling city. Patrols of men armed with pikes paraded the streets. Domiciliary inspections were the only subject of conversation. In my chamber, high up in the roof of the mansion, I could hear the tramp of the armed citizens, the hammering of pikes and the butts of muskets against the neighbouring doors, and the wailing and screaming of the occupants, who were dragged off to the sections. And after the *sans-culottes* had terrorized the peaceable dwellers in the neighbourhood throughout the day, they would assemble in the shop of my neighbour the grocer ; there they would drink, dance the carmagnole, and shriek the *Ça ira* till morning dawned, so that it was impossible for me to close my eyes all night.

o

My uneasiness increased the distress of insomnia. I could not but fear that some valet might have betrayed me, and that my arrest was already ordered.

Just then a fever of denunciation spread through the town. Never a scullion but believed himself a Brutus for the betrayal of the masters who had furnished him with a living.

I was continuously on the alert, and a faithful servant was ready to warn me at the first sound of the knocker. Fully dressed I would throw myself on my bed or into an arm-chair. I carried about with me the key of the small gate in the garden. But as those execrable September days dragged on, when I learned that hundreds of prisoners had been massacred without the least public protest, and under the approving eyes of the magistrates, horror at length got the better of fear in my mind, and I blushed to be taking such precautions for my safety, and defending with so much forethought an existence which the crimes of my country should have rendered worthless.

No longer did I shrink from showing myself in the streets or encountering the patrols. Nevertheless, I clung to life. I possessed a powerful charm against my anguish and grief. One delightful vision banished from my sight the whole sombre panorama which unrolled itself before me. I loved

Amélie, and her youthful countenance omnipresent
to my imagination, held me spell-bound. I loved
without hope. Nevertheless, I seemed to myself less
unworthy of her now that I was acting like a man of
courage. I dared, too, to fancy that the dangers
to which I was exposed might render me more
interesting to her.

In this frame of mind then I went to see her one
morning. I found her alone. She talked to me
with more benignity than she had ever before displayed. Her eyes were cast heavenwards, and
tears fell from them. At the sight I was plunged in
the most indescribable distress. I threw myself
at her feet, seized her hand, and bathed it with
tears.

"O, my brother!" she exclaimed, compelling
me to rise. I had not realized up to that moment
the bitter sweetness the name of brother can
hold. I addressed her with my whole soul's
tenderness.

"Yes," I cried, "the times are frightful. Mankind is steeped in wickedness. Let us away. Happiness is to be sought in solitude. There are still
distant islands where it is possible to live in innocence and freedom from oppression. Let us
depart. We will seek for happiness beneath
the palms that cast their shade over the tomb of
Virginia."

As I talked in this fashion she seemed to be in a dream, and her eyes had a far-away look ; but I could not tell whether her dream and mine were one and the same.

SPENT the rest of the day in the most harrowing suspense. I was powerless either to indulge in rest or to engage in any occupation. Solitude was repellent, and company uncongenial. In this mood I wandered haphazard along the streets and quays of the town, sorrowfully gazing at the mutilated armorial achievements on the fronts of the houses, and at the decapitated saints in the church porches. Thus preoccupied I found myself unconsciously in the garden of the Palais Royal, where a motley crowd of pedestrians had gathered to drink coffee and glance over the gazettes. The wooden galleries, by the way, had not ceased to present a festal appearance at all hours.

In consequence of the declaration of war and the progress of the allied armies, the Parisians had fallen into the habit of seeking for news at the Tuileries and the Palais Royal. In fine weather the crowd would be considerable, and anxiety even brought in its train a certain degree of distraction.

Many of the women, simply attired after the Greek fashion, wore the national colours, either at the waist or in the head-dress. I felt more lonely than ever in this crowd; all the noise, the movement which surrounded me, only served, so to say, to drive back and concentrate my thoughts upon myself.

"Alas!" I said to myself, "have I said enough? Have I shown my feelings unmistakably? Or rather, have I said too much? Will she ever consent to receive me again, now that she knows I love her? But does she know it? and does she care to know it?"

In this fashion I groaned over the uncertainty of my fate, when my attention was violently diverted by the tones of a familiar voice. I raised my eyes and saw Monsieur Mille standing up in a café and singing in the midst of a group of women "patriots" and "citizens." He was dressed as a national guard, and with his left arm he encircled a young woman, in whom I recognized one of the flower-sellers from Ramponneau. To the tune of *Lisette* he was singing these words :—

"Though patriots hundreds strong
To break our bonds are fain,
Women, in thousands, long
To readjust the chain ;

> Tradition holds them fast,
> With pitying scorn they view
> Whoso abhors the past
> And welcomes in the new."[1]

This verse was received with a murmur of approval.   Monsieur Mille smiled, bowed gracefully, and then, turning to his companion, recommenced his song—

> "Ah! not with such join hands,
> Sophie, beloved maid!
> Philosophy's commands
> Yield kindlier, holier aid:
> Her guidance she outpours
> On those—O happy chance!—
> Who to Her rights restores
> Our own, our much wronged France."[2]

---

[1] S'il est douze cents députés
> Qui brisent nos entraves,
> Le vœu de cent mille beautés
> Est de nous rendre esclaves:
> Toutes nos dames ont regret
> A l'ancien régime,
> Et louer un nouveau décret
> C'est perdre leur estime.

[2] Ah! ne les imitez jamais,
> Adorable Sophie,
> Et connaissez mieux les bienfaits
> De la philosophie;
> C'est elle qui dicte les lois
> Aux Solons de la France,
> Et qui fera dans tous ses droits
> Rentrer un peuple immense.

Applause followed, and Monsieur Mille, drawing from his pocket a bunch of ribbons, handed it to Sophie as he resumed his song—

> "Hasten then, far and wide,
>   This gay cockade to show,
> Which fills my breast with pride,
>   When to my guard I go.
> What's gold, with tawdry glint,
>   To the bud which half uncloses?
> This badge of triple tint
>   Outvies the fairest roses." [1]

Sophie fastened the ribbon in her cap, and swept the audience with a glance comprehending both triumph and vacancy. Again there was applause. Monsieur Mille bowed. He gazed at the crowd without recognizing me or anybody else; or, rather, in that crowd he was conscious only of himself.

"Ah! monsieur," exclaimed my neighbour, who in his enthusiasm was bestowing on me a tender embrace; "ah! if the Prussians or the Austrians could see that! They would shudder, monsieur! We were betrayed into their hands at Longwy

---

[1] Hâtez-vouz donc de l'arborer
        Cette belle cocarde,
    Dont j'aime tant à me parer
        Quand je monte ma garde :
    Vous devez préférer à l'or
        Les fleurs à peine écloses ;
    Ce joli ruban tricolor
        A tout l'eclat des roses.

and Verdun. But if they reached Paris it would be their tomb. The spirit of the populace is altogether martial. I have just come from the Tuileries gardens, monsieur. There I heard some singers stationed in front of the statue of Liberty giving voice to the war song of the *Marseillais*. A frenzied crowd was shouting in chorus the refrain ' *Aux armes, citoyens !* ' If the Prussians had only been there ! They would have disappeared underground ! "

The man who thus discoursed to me was a very ordinary person, neither handsome nor ugly, neither short nor tall. He was as like his neighbour as two peas, and there was nothing about him individual or distinctive. As he spoke rather loudly he was soon surrounded. After coughing impressively, he continued—

" The enemy is approaching from Chalons. We must encircle them with a ring of steel. Citizens, it is we who must have an eye to the public welfare. Put not your trust in generals, nor in staff officers and troops of the line, nor in ministers of State, even though you have elected them yourselves ; no, not even in your representatives at the Convention. We must be our own salvation."

" Bravo ! " cried some one in the audience ; " let us fly to Chalons ! "

A little man here made a spirited interruption.

"Patriots have no business to leave Paris until the traitors have been exterminated."

These words were uttered in a voice which I instantly recognized. On that point I could not be deceived. That tremendous head waggling about on a narrow pair of shoulders, that dull livid face, that shape at once mean and monstrous, could belong to none other than my old schoolmaster— Father Joursanvault. His cassock had given place to a wretched jacket. His countenance sweated hate and apostasy. I looked in another direction, but I could not avoid hearing the old Oratorian continue his discourse in this manner :

"Enough blood was not shed during the glorious days of September. The populace is ever too inclined to magnanimity, and has been too tender towards conspirators and traitors."

At these terrible words I took to my heels horror-struck. In my childhood I had suspected Monsieur Joursanvault of being neither just nor benevolent. I disliked him, indeed. But I was far from fathoming the blackness of his soul. At the discovery that my old master was nothing but an unprincipled rascal, I was overwhelmed with mingled bitterness and grief.

"Oh, that I were still but a child!" I exclaimed. "What is the use of life if it cannot bring us to anything better than dilemmas such as this? Dear principal, dear Father Féval, my recollections of you must temper the sorrows that overwhelm me! Into what dangers has the tempest cast you, my dear and only master? This I know, at any rate, that wherever you may be, humanity, pity, and heroism prevail all around you. You taught me, reverend master, the worth of rectitude and courage. You foresaw the days of trial and strengthened my heart. May your pupil, your son, never show himself too unworthy of your care!"

I had hardly concluded this mental invocation when I felt inspired with fresh courage. And my thoughts harking back by a natural inclination to my dear Amélie, I realized all in a moment what my duty was, and resolved to fulfil it. I had disclosed my feelings to Amélie; was I not bound to make the same declaration to Madame Berthemet?

I was only a few paces from the door, for in my self-communing I had naturally drifted towards the house which contained my Amélie. I entered and made my avowal.

Madame Berthemet smilingly replied that my conduct was very praiseworthy. Then, adopting a graver tone, she said—

"I am going to make you my confidant since I cannot otherwise satisfy you. Do not delude yourself; you must abandon all hope. My daughter is beloved by the Chevalier de St. Ange, and I believe that she is not insensible to his devotion. I should be glad enough, however, if she were to dismiss him from her thoughts. For our fortunes are on the wane from day to day, and the Chevalier's love is consequently put to a test which the most ardent sentiments are not always proof against."

The Chevalier de St. Ange! I shuddered at the name. I had a rival, and that rival the most fascinating of poets, the most attractive of novelists. Birth, connections, good looks, talents, he possessed everything calculated to smooth his path. Only the previous evening I had observed in a lady's hands a tortoiseshell box, with a portrait in miniature, mounted on the lid, of the Chevalier de St. Ange, in the uniform of a dragoon.

As I caught sight of it I envied him, as did every other man of his acquaintance, his manly elegance and inimitable grace. Every morning I could hear my neighbour, the mercer's wife, singing at her doorstep the immortal ballad known as *The Pledge*—

> Thou who shouldst never have seen the light,
> Pledge, beloved, that my fault endears;
> Never, ah never, thou luckless wight,
> Frailty of mine to thine eyes bring tears.[1]

> [1] O toi qui n'eus jamais dû naître,
> Gage trop cher d'un fol amour;
> Puisses-tu ne jamais connaître,
> L'erreur qui le donna te jour! (*Le Gage.*)

But a little while since I had been reading with
delight the philosophical romance which opened
the doors of the French Academy to the Chevalier
de St. Ange ; that admirable *Cynégyre* which leaves
far behind it the *Numa Pompilius* of Monsieur
Florian. "Your *Cynégyre*," said the venerable
Monsieur Sedaine to the Chevalier de St. Ange,
as he received him into the illustrious company,
"your *Cynégyre* was dedicated to the manes of
Fénelon, and the offering was not unworthy of the
altar." Such was my rival—the impassioned author
of *The Pledge*—a man of whom people spoke in
one breath with Fénelon and Voltaire ! I could
not overcome my embarrassment ; astonishment
numbed my distress.

"What, Madame ! " I exclaimed, " the Chevalier
de St. Ange ! "

"Yes," rejoined Madame Berthemet, shaking
her head, " a brilliant writer. But do not imagine
for a moment that he is personally the man
you would conjecture from his heroical poems.
Alas ! as our fortunes diminish his love ebbs with
them."

She added kindly that she regretted that her
daughter's choice had not fallen upon me.

"Talents," she said, " do not make for happiness.
On the contrary, men endowed with extraordinary
powers, poets and orators, ought to live single.

What need of companions have they who cannot mate with their equals. Their genius alone is sufficient to foster egoism. One cannot be an eminent man without incurring the penalties."

But I was no longer heedful of her remarks. I could not shake off my astonishment. Her disclosure had killed my love. I had never hoped for its return, and, without hope, love is not endued with any considerable vitality. Mine died at the utterance of a single word.

The Chevalier de St. Ange! Shall I admit it? Although my heart bled, my self-esteem experienced a sort of satisfaction at the thought that, forestalled by such a rival, anybody else, no matter who, would have met the same fate as myself. I pressed a hundred kisses on Madame Berthemet's hands, and left her house calmly, silently, slowly, a mere shadow of the ardent lover who had entered but an hour before, determined to make a clean breast of his scruples and his passion to the mother of Amélie. I was disconsolate. Not that I suffered. I was simply filled with surprise, shame, and fear at the discovery that I could outlive what had seemed the best part of me, my love.

As I crossed the Pont Neuf to regain my deserted faubourg, I saw in the open space, at the foot of the pedestal upon which the statue of Henri IV had recently been erected, a singer from the

Academy of Music, who was declaiming in a moving voice the hymn of the *Marseillais*. The crowd which had collected round him, with bare heads, took up the refrain in chorus, " *Aux armes, citoyens !* " But when the singer struck up the last verse, " *Amour sacré de la Patrie,*" in slow and solemn tones, a shiver of unearthly exaltation passed through the crowd. At the line—

Liberté, liberté chérie . . .

I fell on my knees upon the pavement, and beheld all the people around me likewise fallen prostrate. O, my country, my country ! what spells do you weave that your children worship you so ? Even from out the mire and the blood your image rises radiant. My country ! happy are they who die for you. The sun, which was now dipping towards the horizon, surrounded by blood-hued clouds, lit into liquid flame the waters of the most famous of rivers. Hail to you, ultimate illumination of my days of happiness !

Alack ! into what a winter of discontent I passed that night ! When I closed the door of my little chamber in the roof of the Duc de Puybonne's mansion, I felt as though I were cementing the stone over my own tomb.

"All is over !" I said through my sobs. "I love Amélie no longer. But how is it that I am

forced to remind myself of the fact so untiringly?
How is it that, loving her no longer, I cannot turn
my thoughts away from her? Why do I lament
so bitterly the uprooting of my wretched love?"

Cruel anxieties were added to my personal
sorrows. The state of public affairs was driving
me to desperation. My destitution was extreme,
and, far from cherishing the hope of obtaining
work, I was reduced to concealing myself for fear
of being arrested as a suspicious character.

Monsieur Mille had not put in an appearance at
the house since the 10th of August. I have no
idea where he lodged; but he never missed a
single sitting of the Commune, and every day
before the municipality, amid enthusiastic applause
from the *tricoteuses* [1] and *sans-culottes,* he would recite
a new patriotic hymn. Indeed he was the most
patriotic of poets, and citizen Dorat-Cubières himself, beside him, was a timid *Feuillant,* [2] under the
grave suspicion of the demagogues. I had been
engaged in incriminating transactions; moreover,
Monsieur Mille made no attempt to visit me, and

[1] The women who formed part of the revolutionary mobs were
known as *tricoteuses* from their habit of knitting at all seasons, even
at the foot of the guillotine; the *sans-culottes* were the men of the
same class. Their nether garments, of course, were rather in rags
and tatters than wanting altogether. (TRANS.)

[2] A member of an anti-Jacobin Society, known as *Feuillants.*
(TRANS.)

my own scruples made it an easy duty for me not to
go in search of him. Nevertheless, being a good-
hearted man, he sent me his collection of songs when
the printing was completed. Ah, how slight the resemblance between his second muse and his first!
The latter had been powdered, painted, perfumed.
The new one resembled a fury, with serpents for
locks of hair. I can still recall the song of the *sans-
culottes*, which aimed at being very malicious. It
began thus—

> Long, long enough, yea far too long
> Dread tyranny has claimed our song,
>   And despots swayed our lot.
> Now breaks the dawn of Liberty,
> Of Law, and fair Equality:
>   All hail! the Sans-Culottes![1]

The trial of the king aroused me to indescribable
distress. My days rolled by in horror. One
morning there was a knock at the door. I divined
somehow that it proceeded from a gentle and
friendly hand. I opened, and Madame Berthemet
flung herself into my arms.

"Save me, save us!" she said. "My brother,

---

[1] Amis, assez et trop longtemps,
    Sous le règne affreux des tyrans,
        On chanta les despotes.
    Sous celui de l'Egalité,
    Des Lois et de la Liberté,
        Chantons les Sans-Culottes.

Monsieur Eustance, my only brother, was scheduled as an *émigré*,[1] and came to seek shelter in my house. He was denounced and arrested. He has been in prison now for five days. Luckily the accusation which hangs over him is vague and ill-founded. My brother was never an *émigré*. To effect his release, all that is necessary is that some one who can vouch for his unbroken residence in France will give evidence in his favour. I begged the Chevalier de St. Ange to do me this service. He prudently begged to be excused. Well! my friend, my son, that service which it would be perilous to him to render me, to you will be still more perilous; yet I come to ask it of you."

I thanked her for her request as if it had been a favour. And, indeed, it was so to be regarded, and of a quality so inestimable that an upright man could scarcely be honoured by a greater.

"Well enough I knew that you would not refuse!" exclaimed Madame Berthemet, embracing me. "But this is not all," she added. "You will need to procure a second witness; they demand that two shall come forward if my brother is to be released. Oh, my friend, what times we are living in! Monsieur de St. Ange keeps aloof from us; our misfortunes embarrass him; and Monsieur

[1] A person who had left France without a licence from the Government. (Trans.)

Mille would be afraid to visit folks under suspicion. Who would have thought it, my friend—
who would have thought it? Do you remember
Federation Day? We were all brimful of enthusiasm about fraternity, and I had on a very
becoming dress."

She was in tears when she left me. I descended
the stairs almost immediately after her to go in
search of a guarantor, and to tell the truth I was
considerably puzzled to put my hands on one. As
I bowed my head in my hands I realized that I
had a beard of eight days' growth, which might
render me an object of suspicion; so I betook
myself at once to my barber's at the corner of the
Rue St. Guillaume. This barber was a very
worthy fellow named Larisse, as tall as a poplar and
as restless as an aspen. When I entered his shop
he was attending to a wine merchant of the neighbourhood, who with his face smothered in lather
was pouring out all sorts of playful threats.

"Ah, my fine fellow, you dandifier of fine ladies,"
he was saying, "your head will be cut off and
stuck on the end of a pike to gratify your aristo-
cratic inclinations. Every enemy of the people
must add his quota to the basket,[1] from the fat
Capet to the slim Larisse. And, ça ira, so it will
be!"

---

[1] The basket into which the heads of the guillotined fell. (TRANS.)

Monsieur Larisse, paler than moonshine and fluttering like a leaf, observed the utmost precautions as he shaved the chin of the abusive patriot. I can affirm that never did barber experience greater terror. And from this circumstance I drew a happy augury for the success of the design I had suddenly conceived. It was my intention, to be plain, to ask Monsieur Larisse to accompany me before the committee as the second guarantor.

"He is such a coward," I reflected, "that he will never dare to protest."

The wine merchant withdrew muttering fresh threats, and left me alone with the barber, who, still trembling, fastened a napkin round my neck.

"Ah, monsieur!" he whispered in my ear, in a voice feebler than a sigh, "hell is let loose upon us! Was it for the accommodation of demons like this that I studied the art of hairdressing? The heads which did honour to my skill are now in London or in Coblentz. How is Monseigneur le Duc de Puybonne? He was a good master."

I informed him that the Duke was living in London, and giving writing lessons. Indeed, the Duke had managed recently to convey to me a paper in which he told me that he was living, perfectly contented, in London, on four shillings and sixpence a day.

"It may be so," replied Monsieur Larisse, "but

in London hairdressing is not performed as it is in Paris. The English can make constitutions, but they don't know how to make wigs, and their powder is not nearly white enough."

Monsieur Larisse soon had me shaven. I had not a very harsh beard at that time. Scarcely had he closed his razor than, seizing him by the wrist, I said to him firmly—

"My dear Monsieur Larisse, you are a valiant man; you are coming with me before the General Assembly of the Section des Postes in the one-time church of St. Eustache. There you will bear witness jointly with me that Monsieur Eustance has never been an *émigré*."

At these words Monsieur Larisse grew pale, and murmured in inanimate tones—

"But I am not acquainted with Monsieur Eustance."

"For that matter, neither am I," I replied.

Which was indeed strictly true. I had correctly diagnosed the character of Monsieur Larisse. He was dumbfounded. His very fear thrust him into the perilous emprise. I took him by the arm and he followed me unresistingly.

"But you are leading me to my death," he said softly.

"To glory rather," I replied.

I don't know whether he was familiar with the

tragedians, but he was sensible of the honour and appeared flattered. He had some knowledge of literature, for loosing my arm to go into his back shop, he said—

"A moment, dear sir ; let me at least put on my best coat. In the olden times the victims were decked with flowers. I find it recorded in the *Almanack for Honest Men*."

From his chest of drawers he took a blue coat which he flung round his long, mobile body. Thus attired he accompanied me to the General Assembly of the Section des Postes, which was sitting continuously.

On the threshold of the desecrated church, on the door of which was inscribed the motto, "*Liberty, Equality, Fraternity, or Death,*" Monsieur Larisse felt the sweat break out on his forehead ; nevertheless he went in. One of the citizens who was sleeping there on a heap of empty bottles, half aroused himself to inquire our business, and then sent us on to the revolutionary committee of the Section.

I knew this committee through having accompanied Monsieur Berthemet there on two occasions. The president of it was a small lodging-house keeper in the Rue de la Truanderie, whose most regular customers were ladies of easy virtue. Amongst the members there were an itinerant knife-grinder, a porter, and a dyer and cleaner named Bistac. It was with the knife-grinder that we had to do. He was seated informally with his sleeves turned up ; we found him a good-natured fellow.

"Citizens," he said, "from the moment you place before me an attestation in due form, I have no objections to raise, because I am a magistrate and consequently the proper formalities are all I demand. I would only add one word. A man who has intelligence and character ought not to be authorized to leave Paris at a moment like this. Because, you see, citizens——"

He hesitated, and then, making use of gesture to express his meaning, he stretched out his bare and muscular arm and then moved it to his forehead, which he tapped with a finger, and continued—
" It is not of this alone" (here he indicated his arm, the working tool) " that we have need, but of this also " (here he motioned to his forehead, the seat of intellect).

He then boasted of his natural gifts, and lamented that his parents had not contrived to give him any instruction. Then he set himself to the task of signing our declaration. Despite his good will this was a long process. Whilst, with hands accustomed to the grindstone, he painfully manipulated the pen, Bistac the cleaner came into the room. Bistac had not the genial nature of the grinder. His soul was all Jacobin. At sight of us his forehead puckered and his nostrils swelled : he scented the aristocrat.

"Who are you ?" he demanded of me.

"Pierre Aubier."

"Oh, oh ! Pierre Aubier, and I suppose you flatter yourself that you will sleep in your own bed to-night ?"

I put a cool face on the situation, but my companion began to shudder in every limb. His bones rattled so loudly that Bistac's attention was attracted, and, forgetting me, he turned his scrutiny on to poor Larisse.

"You have all the marks of a conspirator, in my opinion," said Bistac in a terrible voice. "What is your profession ?"

"A barber, at your service, citizen."

"All barbers are Feuillants ! "

Terror commonly inspired Monsieur Larisse to the most courageous actions. He has since confessed to me that at this moment he had all the difficulty in the world to prevent himself from shouting "Long live the King ! " As a matter of fact, he did no such thing, but replied proudly that he owed small thanks to the Revolution, which had suppressed wigs and powder, and that he was tired of living in a continual state of apprehension.

"Take off my head," he added. "I should prefer to get my dying over, rather than to live in constant fear."

Bistac became perplexed at talk like this.

Meanwhile, the knife-grinder, who was revolving many confused but kindly thoughts in his brain, recommended us to withdraw.

"Off with you, citizens," he said; "but bear in mind that the Republic has need of this."

And he pointed to his forehead.

Madame Berthemet's brother was released next day. The mother of Amélie expressed abundance of gratitude and embraced me—it was a way she had. She did better.

"You have," said she, "acquired a right to the gratitude of Amélie. I am desirous that my daughter should herself come and express her indebtedness to you. She owes you an uncle. It is less than a mother, it is true; but what commendations does not your courage deserve. . . ."

She went in search of Amélie.

Left alone in the drawing-room, I waited. I asked myself whether I had the strength to see her once more. I feared, I hoped. I died a thousand deaths.

In about five minutes Madame Berthemet reappeared, alone.

"You must excuse an ungrateful girl," she said.

" My daughter refuses to come. 'I could not endure his presence,' she declared. 'The sight of him would be torture to me; henceforth I hate him. By showing greater courage than the man I love, he has gained a cruel advantage. I will never see him again while I live. He is generous : he will forgive me.' "

After she had repeated this speech to me Madame Berthemet concluded with these words :

" Forget the ungrateful child ! "

I promised to endeavour to do so, and I kept my word. Events contributed to my success. The Terror reigned. That appalling day, the 31st of May, snatched their last hopes from those of the moderate party.

Several times I was denounced as a conspirator on the score of the correspondence I maintained with the Duc de Puybonne, and I was continually risking both liberty and life.

I had no longer a certificate of citizenship, and, not daring to apply for one for fear of being instantly put under arrest, my existence had become unendurable.

There was a demand just then for twelve hundred thousand men between the ages of eighteen and twenty-five. I entered my name. On the 7th of Brumaire in the year II, at six o'clock in the morning, I set out on the way to Nancy to join my regiment. With a policeman's cap on my head, a knapsack on my back, and wearing the jacket called a carmagnole, I felt myself fairly martial in appearance.

From time to time I turned my gaze back on the great city where I had suffered so much and loved so profoundly. Then, wiping away a tear, I resumed my journey. I decided to sing in order to cheer myself up, and I began the hymn of the *Marseillais*—

Allons, enfants de la Patrie!

At the first halting-place I presented my credentials to some peasants, who sent me to pass the night in the stable on the straw. There I enjoyed a delicious sleep, and as I awakened I thought—

"Well, this is better. I am no longer in danger of the guillotine. So far as I can judge, I am no longer in love with Amélie—or rather I never have been in love with her. I am going to carry a sword and a gun. I shall have nothing else to fear but the Austrian bullets. Brindamour and Trompelamort are right: there is no finer calling than that of a soldier. But who would have dreamed when I was studying Latin under the flowering apple trees at Monsieur Lamadou's that one day I should take arms in defence of the Republic? Ah! Monsieur Féval, who could have foreseen that your little pupil Pierre would march away to the wars?"

At the next halt a worthy woman put me to sleep in white sheets because I reminded her of her son.

The following day I lodged with a canoness who put me in a loft open to the wind and rain, and even this she did with a very perturbed mind, for a defender of the Republic seemed to her so very near to a dangerous species of brigand.

Finally, I came up with my corps on the banks of the Meuse. I received a sword. At this I reddened with gratification, and felt myself at least a foot taller. Do not laugh at me on that account; it was a case of vanity, I admit it; but vanity goes to the making of a hero. We were scarcely fitted out before we received orders to start for Maubeuge.

We arrived on the Sambre on a dark night. Silence was all around. We could see fires flickering on the hills on the opposite side of the river. I was told that they were the bivouacs of the enemy. Then my heart thumped as if it would burst.

It was from Titus Livy that I had got my ideas of war. But I call you to witness, woods, meadows, hills, banks of the Sambre and the Meuse, that those ideas were delusive. War, such as I took part in, consists of passing through burnt-up villages, sleeping in the mire, listening to the whistle of bullets through the long and melancholy sentry duty of nights ; but of single combats and ordered battlefields I saw never a sign. We slept but little, and did not eat at all. Floridor, my sergeant, an old soldier of the French Guard, swore that the life we were leading was festive ; he exaggerated, but we were not unhappy, for we had the conscious-ness of doing our duty and being useful to our country.

We were justly proud of our regiment, which had covered itself with glory at Wattignies. For the greater part it was made up of soldiers of the old *régime*, stout and well instructed. As a large number of men had perished in various engage-ments, the gaps had been filled up anyhow with youthful recruits. Without the veterans who encircled us we should have been worth nothing. It takes a good deal of time to make a soldier, and in war enthusiasm is no substitute for expe-rience.

My colonel was a one-time nobleman from my native province. He treated me kindly. A life-long Royalist, a countryman not a townsman, a soldier not a courtier, he had long delayed ex-changing the white coat of His Majesty's troops for the blue coat of the soldiers of the year II. He detested the Republic, and dedicated the remainder of his life to it.

I bless Providence for having guided me to the frontier, since there virtue still survives.

[Written in bivouac, on the Sambre, between septidi the 27th of Frimaire, and sextidi the 6th of Nivôse, in the year II of the French Republic, by Pierre Aubier, volunteer.]

DAWN

TO MADEMOISELLE LEONIE BERNARDINI

DAWN

THE Cours-La-Reine was deserted. The green banks of the Seine, the ancient pollarded beeches whose shadows began to stretch out towards the east, the calm azure of the sky, cloudless, breezeless, unthreatening but unsmiling, all were wrapped in the deep silence that marks the summer day. A pedestrian coming from the Tuileries made his way slowly towards the hills of Chaillot. His figure was of the agreeable slightness characteristic of early youth, and he wore the coat, breeches, and black stockings indicative of the bourgeois, whose supremacy had at length come round. Yet his countenance was rather that of the dreamer than of the enthusiast. He had a book in his hand; and his finger between the leaves marked the place he had reached, but he had ceased to read. Now and then he stopped and strained his ears to catch the faint yet terrible murmur which rose up from Paris, and in this muffled noise, feebler than a sigh, he fancied he could distinguish cries of death and hate, joy and love, drum-beats, the sound

of firearms—all the din, in fact, of insensate fury
and sublime enthusiasm which ascends heavenward
from crowded streets at the outbreak of revolution.
At times he turned his head and shuddered. Everything reported to him, everything he had seen and
heard for some hours past filled his brain with
confused and terrible pictures : the Bastille captured
by the people and already denuded of its battle-
ments ; the provost of the merchants' guild slain
by a pistol-shot in the midst of a furious crowd ;
the governor, the venerable de Launay, hewn down
on the steps of the Hôtel de Ville ; the dreadful
populace, pale as famine or as deathly fear, drunken,
beside itself, dazed by the vision of blood and
glory, reeling from the Bastille to the Grève, and
above the heads of a hundred thousand deluded
people the bodies of the victims swinging from a
lamp-post, and the oak-crowned brow of one of the
exultant clad in a uniform of blue and white ; the
conquerors with the registers, the keys and the
silver plate belonging to the ancient fortress, mount-
ing amid acclamation the blood-stained steps ; and
at their head the popular magistrates La Fayette
and Bailly, overwrought, uplifted, amazed, their
feet dabbled in blood, their heads touching the
clouds with pride ! Then, fear still paramount
with the unleashed rabble, at the scattered noises
customarily attendant on the return of the Royal

troops to the town at night, the tearing down of
the palace railings for conversion into pikes, the
pillage of the arsenals, the construction by the
citizens of street barricades, and the transportation
by the women to the roofs of houses of stones to
hurl down on the foreign regiments !

These scenes of violence were reconstructed in
his dreamy youthful imagination in subdued tones.
He had taken his favourite book, an English work
entited *Meditations Among the Tombs*, and made his
way along the Seine, under the trees of the Cours-
la-Reine, towards the white house which, night and
day, filled his thoughts. All was calm around him.
On the river bank he noticed the anglers sitting
with their feet in the water, and he followed the
course of the stream in an abstracted mood. When
he reached the slopes of the hills of Chaillot he
met a patrol party, keeping an eye on the com-
munications between Paris and Versailles. This
troop, armed with guns, muskets, and halberds,
included artisans wearing their aprons of leather or
serge, lawyers dressed in black, one priest, and a
bearded, bare-legged giant in a shirt. They chal-
lenged every would-be passer-by : communica-
tions between the Court and the governor of the
Bastille had been detected and a surprise was
feared.

But this pedestrian was young and of ingenuous

appearance. He had scarcely uttered a word or two before the troop smilingly permitted him to continue his journey.

He ascended the slope of a lane odorous of flowering elder, and stopped half-way up in front of a garden gate. This garden was but little, but by means of winding alleys and abrupt turns the space for exercise was considerably extended. Into a pool where ducks were disporting themselves, willows dipped the tips of their branches. At the corner by the street a light alcove had been constructed, and a grass plot spread its freshness in front of the house. Here, on a rustic bench, with her head bent, a young woman was seated; her face was hidden by a large straw hat wreathed with natural flowers. Over her dress, which was of white and rose colour, in stripes, she wore a fichu, fastened at the waistline, this latter a trifle high, giving the skirt an added length that was not unbecoming. Her arms, encased in tight sleeves, were at rest. A basket of an antique pattern, which lay at her feet, held balls of wool. Close by her a child was piling up heaps of sand with his shovel. His blue eyes shone through a tangle of golden hair.

The young woman remained motionless and, as it were, spell-bound, and the young man standing at the gate could not bring himself to break so sweet a spell. At length she raised her head and disclosed a youthful, almost infantile face, with pure rounded lines which imparted a natural expression of gentleness and friendliness. He bowed before her, and she held out her hand.

"How do you do, Monsieur Germain? What is the news? 'What news do you bring with you?' as the song says. I don't know very much, except songs."

"Pardon me, Madame, for having disturbed your dreams. I was gazing at you. Alone, motionless, your head resting on your hand, it seemed as though you must be the angel of meditation."

"Alone! alone!" she replied, as if this were the only word she had heard. "Alone! Is she ever alone?"

And seeing that he was looking at her uncomprehendingly, she added—

"Enough of that! It is nothing but a fancy of mine that—— What is your news?"

Thereupon he went over the events of the famous day, the taking of the Bastille, the foundation of liberty.

Sophie listened to him gravely; then she said—

"It is our duty to rejoice, but our joy should be the austere joy which comes of sacrifice. Henceforth the French are their own men no longer;

they are the servants of the Revolution which is about to reform the world."

As she was speaking the child approached and threw himself joyously across her knees.

"Look, mamma! Look at my pretty garden!"

Embracing him, she said—

"You are right, little Emile, it is the wisest thing in the world to lay out a pretty garden."

"Yes, he is right," added Germain; "what gallery glowing with porphyry and gold can be compared with a green alley?"

And reflecting how sweet it would be to give this fair woman the support of his arm and lead her to the shade of the trees—

"Ah!" he exclaimed, flashing a meaning glance at her, "what are men and revolutions to me!"

"No, no!" she rejoined, "I cannot so abruptly turn my thoughts from a great people, intent on inaugurating the reign of justice. My attachment to the new ideas surprises you, Monsieur Germain. We have only known one another for quite a brief time. You are not aware, of course, that my father taught me to read in the *Social Contract* and the Gospels. One day, as we were walking, he pointed out Jean Jacques Rousseau to me. I was only a child, but I dissolved in tears at sight of the gloomy countenance of the wisest of men. I grew up a hater of prejudice. Later on my husband, like myself a disciple of the philosophy of nature, decided that our son should be called Emile, and that he should be taught to labour with his hands. In his last letter, written three years ago on board the ship upon which he perished some days afterwards, he continues to urge on my attention Rousseau's precepts upon education. I am saturated with the new spirit of the age. It is my conviction that we must struggle for justice and truth."

"Like yourself, Madame," sighed Germain, "I have a horror of fanaticism and tyranny; like yourself, I am in love with liberty, but my soul is drained of its strength. At every moment my thoughts escape my control. I am no longer master of myself, and I suffer accordingly."

The young woman did not reply. An elderly man pushed open the gate and came forward with his arms raised, waving his hat. He wore neither powder nor wig. A few long grey hairs fell down on each side of his bald head. He wore a complete suit of grey ratteen; his stockings were blue and his shoes buckleless.

"Victory! victory!" he cried. "The monster is delivered into our hands, Sophie, and I am the bearer of the news to you."

"Neighbour, I have just heard of it from Monsieur Marcel Germain, whom I want to introduce to you. His mother and mine were friends at Angers. During the six months he has spent in Paris he has been kind enough to come to see me from time to time in the seclusion of my hermitage. Monsieur Germain, this gentleman is my neighbour and friend, Monsieur Franchot de La Cavanne, a man of letters."

"Say rather, 'Nicolas Franchot, labourer.'"

"I know, dear friend, that you thus signed your treatise on the Corn Trade. I will say then, to gratify you, although I expect your hands are much more adroit with the pen than with the plough, Monsieur Nicolas Franchot, labourer."

The older man grasped Marcel's hand and exclaimed—

"It has fallen, then, that fortress which has so many times engulfed the wronged and the guiltless ! Those bolts behind which I passed eight months, deprived both of air and light, have been torn from their places. It was one-and-thirty years ago, on the 17th of February, 1758, that I was cast into the Bastille for having written an epistle on tolerance. Now, to-day, at length the people have avenged me. Right and I are triumphant together. The memory of this day will remain so long as the universe endures. I call as witness to it the sun which saw Harmodius perish, and the brood of Tarquin put to flight !"

The piercing voice of Monsieur Franchot frightened little Emile, who clutched his mother's dress. Franchot, suddenly becoming aware of the child's presence, lifted him from the ground and said enthusiastically—

"Happier than we have been, dear child, you will grow up free !"

But Emile, terrified, turned his face away and uttered loud cries.

"Gentlemen," said Sophie, as she wiped away her little son's tears, "will you be so kind as to stay to supper with me ? I am expecting Monsieur Duvernay, provided he is not detained by the bedside of one of his patients."

Then turning towards Marcel—

"You must know that Monsieur Duvernay, the king's physician, is an elector of Paris without the walls. He would be a deputy of the National Assembly if, like Monsieur de Condorcet, he had not out of modesty declined the honour. He is a man of great attainments, and it will be both pleasant and profitable to you to hear him converse."

"Young man," added Franchot, "I am acquainted with Monsieur Jean Duvernay, and I know one circumstance about him which does him honour. Two years ago the queen summoned him to attend on the Dauphin, who was threatened with decline.

At that time Duvernay was residing at Sèvres, whither one of the Court carriages was sent every morning to convey him to Saint Cloud, where the royal child lay ill. One day the carriage returned to the palace empty. Duvernay had not come. The following day the queen reproached him for absenting himself.

"Doctor," she said, "you forgot your patient the Dauphin, then?"

"Madame," replied the worthy man, "I am caring for your son assiduously, but yesterday I was detained by the bedside of a peasant woman in labour."

"Well now!" remarked Sophie, "wasn't that noble of him, and oughtn't we to be proud of our friend!"

"Yes; it was fine," replied Germain.

A grave, sweet voice close beside them here interposed—

"I do not know," said the voice, "what it is that is exciting you to admiration; but it is pleasant to hear your transports. In these days there are so many admirable deeds to be witnessed."

The man who spoke wore a powdered wig and a delicate lace frill. It was Jean Duvernay. Marcel recognized his face from the engravings he had seen in the shops in the Palais Royal.

"I have just come from Versailles," said Duvernay. "I owe to the Duke of Orleans the pleasure of seeing you this memorable day, Sophie. He brought me in his coach as far as Saint Cloud. The rest of the way I travelled in the most convenient fashion—I mean on my own feet."

And as a matter of fact, his silver-buckled shoes and black stockings were covered all over with dust.

Emile clung with his little hands to the steel buttons which glittered on the doctor's coat, and Duvernay, coaxing him on to his knee, found material for smiles in glimpses at the little creature's budding soul. Sophie summoned Nanon. A sturdy girl appeared, who picked up and carried the child off in her arms, stifling beneath resounding kisses his despairing cries.

The table was laid in the garden alcove. Sophie hung her straw hat on a willow branch ; her fair hair fell in curls about her cheeks.

"You will sup in the simplest possible way," she said, "in the English fashion."

From the spot where they were seated they could see the Seine, the roofs of the city, the domes and the steeples. The spectacle rendered them as silent as though they were looking out on Paris for the first time. After a while they spoke of the occurrences of the day, of the Assembly, of universal suffrage, of the breaking down of class barriers, and

Monsieur Necker's banishment. All four were agreed that a lasting liberty was at length achieved. Monsieur Duvernay foretold the rise of a new order, and applauded the wisdom of the legislators popularly elected. But his mind was not uplifted, and at times it seemed as though his hopes were alloyed with a certain uneasiness. Nicolas Franchot did not observe the same moderation. He proclaimed the peaceful triumph of the people and the era of fraternity.

Vainly did the physician, vainly the young woman assure him—

"It is only now that the struggle begins. We are only as yet at our first victory."

"Philosophy is our ruler," he would reply. "What benefits will not Reason shower on men who accept her all potent sway! The Golden Age which the poets fabled will become a reality. All ills will disappear with the fanaticism and tyranny which gave them birth. The virtuous and enlightened man will enjoy all possible felicity. What do I say? By the aid of physicians and chemists he will even succeed in attaining immortality upon earth."

Sophie listened to him, but shook her head.

"If you wish to deprive us of death," she said, "find us first a fountain of youth. Without that your immortality awakens my apprehension."

The old philosopher laughingly asked her if she found the Christian doctrine of resurrection more comforting.

"For my part," he said, after emptying his glass, "I am inclined to fear lest the angels and saints should feel impelled to favour the choir of virgins at the expense of the company of dowagers."

"I do not know," replied the young woman, in a meditative tone and lifting her eyes to his, "I do not know what value these poor charms, framed out of the dust of the earth, may have in the eyes of angels ; but I am sure that divine omnipotence will be better able to repair the ravages of time, if in so blissful an abode such redress should be needful, than all your physics and your chemistry will ever succeed in doing in this world. You, who are an atheist, Monsieur Franchot, and do not believe that God reigns in the heavens, you cannot understand anything about the Revolution, which is the advent of God upon earth."

She rose. Night had fallen, and in the distance under their eyes the great town starred itself with lights.

Marcel offered his arm to Sophie, and whilst the older men argued with one another, the two sauntered together along the sombre alleys. Marcel found them charming, and Sophie supplied him in turn with their names and associations.

"Here," she said, "we are in the Allée de Jean Jacques, which leads to the Salon d'Emile. This alley was straight. I had it deflected so that it should pass under the old oak. All day long it gives shade to this rustic bench, which I have called 'Friendship's Rest.'

"We will sit down for a moment on this bench," said Sophie.

They sat down. In the silence Marcel could hear the fluttering of his own heart.

"Sophie, I love you," he murmured, and captured her hand.

She drew it away gently, and pointing out to the young man that a light breeze had set the leaves rustling—

"Do you hear that?" she said.

"I hear the wind among the leaves."

She shook her head, and said in tones as sweet as a chant—

"Marcel, Marcel! Who tells you that is the wind among the leaves? Who tells you that we are alone? Are you, then, after all, one of those commonplace souls which have failed to discern any of the mysterious portents of the world unseen?"

And as he questioned her with a glance that was all bewilderment—

"Monsieur Germain," she said, "be so kind

as to go upstairs to my room. You will find a little book on the table, and bring it to me . . ."

He obeyed. All the while he was absent the young widow gazed at the dusky foliage shivering in the night wind. He returned with a little gilt-edged volume.

" *The Idylls of Gesner;* yes, that is it," said Sophie. "Open the book at the place where the marker lies, and, if your eyes are good enough to read by moonlight, read."

He read these words:

" Ah! Often will my soul come to hover around you; often when, inflamed by a noble and sublime thought, you are meditating in solitude, a light breath will brush your cheek: at such a moment may your soul be conscious of a gladdening thrill! . . ."

She stopped him.

" Now do you understand, Marcel, that we are never alone, and that there are words to which I can never listen so long as a breath blown landward from the sea shall set in motion the leaves of the oaks."

The voices of the two older men drew near.

" God is Goodness," said Duvernay.

" God is evil," said Franchot, " and we shall extinguish it."

Both of them, and Marcel also, took leave of Sophie.

"Adieu, gentlemen," she said. "Let us all cry, 'Hurrah for Liberty, and long live the King!' And you, dear neighbour, do not hinder us from dying when we shall need to die."

MADAME DE LUZY

TO MARCEL PROUST

MADAME DE LUZY

(From a manuscript dated September 15th, 1792.)

I

S I entered, Pauline de Luzy held out her hand to me. Then for a moment we remained silent. Her scarf and straw hat were thrown carelessly on an arm-chair.

The prayer from *Orpheus* was open on the spinet. Going towards the window, she watched the sun sinking to the blood-red horizon.

"Madame," I said at length, "do you remember the words you said two years ago this very day, at the foot of that hill on the bank of the river towards which at this moment your eyes are turned?

"Do you remember how, with your hand waving in a prophetic gesture, you called up before me, as in a vision, the coming days of trial, of crime and terror? On my very lips you arrested my confession of love, and bade me live and labour for justice and liberty. Madame, since your hand, which I

243

could not anoint with kisses and tears enough, pointed out the way to me, I have pursued it unfaltering. I have obeyed you ; I have written and spoken for the cause. For two years I have withstood the blunder-headed starvelings who are the source of dissension and hate, the demagogues who seduce the people by violent demonstrations of pretended sympathy, and the poltroons who do homage to the coming powers."

She stopped me with a motion of her hand, and made a sign to me to listen. Then we heard borne across the scented spaces of the garden, where birds were warbling, distant cries of " Death ! " " To the gallows with the aristocrat ! " " Set his head on a pike ! "

Pale and motionless she held a finger to her lips.

" It is," I said, " some unhappy wretch being pursued. They are making domiciliary visits and effecting arrests in Paris night and day. It is possible they may force an entrance here. I ought to withdraw for fear of compromising you. Although I am but little known in this neighbourhood, I am, as times go, a dangerous guest."

" Stay ! " she adjured me.

For the second time cries rent the calm evening air. They were mingled now with the tramp of feet and the noise of fire-arms. They came nearer ;

then we heard a voice shout : " Close the approaches, so that he cannot escape, the scoundrel ! "

Madame de Luzy seemed to grow calmer in proportion to the increasing nearness of the danger.

" Let us go up to the second floor," she said ; " we shall be able to see through the sunblinds what is going on outside."

But scarcely had we opened the door when, on the landing, we beheld a half-dressed fugitive, his face blanched with terror, his teeth chattering and his knees knocking together. This apparition murmured in a strangled voice—

" Save me ! Hide me ! They are there. . . . They burst open my gate—overran my garden. They are coming. . . ."

ADAME DE LUZY, recognizing Planchonnet, the old philosopher who occupied the neighbouring house, asked him in a whisper—

"Has my cook caught sight of you? She is a Jacobin!"

"Nobody has set eyes on me."

"God be praised, neighbour!"

She led him into her bedroom, whither I followed them. A consultation was necessary. Some hiding-place must be hit upon where she could keep Planchonnet concealed for several days, or at least for several hours, whatever time it might take to deceive and tire out the search party. It was agreed that I should keep the approaches under observation, and that when I gave the signal, the unfortunate man should make his escape by the little garden gate.

Whilst he waited, he was unable to remain standing. He was completely paralysed with terror.

He endeavoured to make us understand that he was being hounded down for having conspired with Monsieur de Cazotte against the Constitution, and for having on the 10th of August formed one of the defenders of the Tuileries—he, the enemy of priests and kings. It was an infamous calumny. The truth was that Lubin was venting his hate upon him—Lubin, hitherto his butcher, whom he had a hundred times had a mind to lay a stick about to teach him to give better weight, and who was now presiding over the section in which he had formerly been a mere stallholder.

As he uttered the name in strangled tones, he was persuaded that he actually saw Lubin, and hid his face in his hands. And of a truth there was the sound of footsteps on the stairs. Madame de Luzy shot the bolts and pushed the old man behind a screen. There was a hammering at the door, and Pauline recognized the voice of her cook, who called out to her to open, that the municipal officers were at the gate with the National Guard, and that they had come to make an inspection of the premises.

"They say," the woman added, "that Planchonnet is in the house. I know very well that it is not so, of course. I know you would never harbour a scoundrel of that sort; but they won't believe my word."

"Well, well, let them come up," replied Madame de Luzy through the door. "Let them go all over the house, from cellar to garret."

As he listened to this dialogue, the wretched Planchonnet fainted behind the screen, and I had a good deal of trouble in resuscitating him by sprinkling water on his temples. When I had succeeded—

"My friend," the young woman whispered to her old neighbour, "trust in me. Remember that women are resourceful."

Then, calmly, as though she had been engaged in some daily domestic duty, she drew her bedstead a little out from its alcove, took off the bedclothes, and with my assistance so arranged the three mattresses as to contrive a space next the wall between the highest and the lowest of them.

Whilst she was making these arrangements, a loud noise of shoes, sabots, gunstocks, and raucous voices broke out on the staircase. This was for all three of us a terrible moment; but the noise ascended by little and little to the floor above our heads. We realized that the searchers, under the guidance of the Jacobin cook, were ransacking the garrets first. The ceiling cracked; threats and coarse laughter were audible, and the sound of kicks and bayonet-thrusts against the wainscot. We breathed again, but there was not a second to lose. I helped Planchonnet to slip into the space contrived for him between the mattresses.

As she watched our efforts, Madame de Luzy

shook her head. The bed thus disturbed had a suspicious appearance.

She endeavoured to give it a finishing touch ; but in vain, she could not make it look natural.

"I shall have to go to bed myself," she said.

She looked at the clock ; it was exactly seven, and she felt that it would look extraordinary for her to be in bed so early. As to feigning illness, it was useless to think of it : the Jacobin cook would detect the ruse.

She remained thoughtful for some seconds ; then calmly, simply, with royal unconcern, she undressed before me, got into bed, and ordered me to take off my shoes, my coat, and my cravat.

"There is nothing for it but for you to be my lover, and for them to surprise us together. When they arrive you will not have had time to re-arrange your disordered clothes. You will open the door to them in your vest,[1] with your hair rumpled."

All our arrangements were made when the search party, with many exclamations of " *Sacré !* " and " *Peste !* " descended from the garrets.

The unfortunate Planchonnet was seized with such a paroxysm of trembling that he shook the whole bed.

[1] The vest was worn under the coat. It was a sort of waistcoat, longer than ours, and provided with sleeves of full length. (AUTHOR.)

Moreover, his breathing grew so stertorous that it must have been almost audible in the corridor.

"It's a pity," murmured Madame de Luzy. "I was so satisfied with my little artifice. But never mind ; we won't despair. May God be our aid !"

A heavy fist shook the door.

"Who knocks ?" Pauline inquired.

"The representatives of the Nation."

"Can't you wait a minute ?"

"Open, or we shall break the door down !"

"Go and open the door, my friend."

Suddenly, by a sort of miracle, Planchonnet ceased to tremble and gasp.

UBIN was the first to enter. He had his scarf round him, and was followed by a dozen men armed with pikes. Casting his eyes first on Madame de Luzy and then on me—

"*Peste !*" he exclaimed. "It seems we are disturbing a pair of lovers. Excuse us, pretty one !"

Then turning to his followers, he remarked—

"The *sans-culottes* are the only folks who know how to behave."

But despite his theories this e counter had evidently put him in good spirits.

He sat down on the bed, and raising the chin of the lovely high-bred woman, said—

"It is plain that that pretty mouth wasn't made to mumble paternosters day and night. It would have been a pity if it were. But the Republic before all things. We are seeking the traitor, Planchonnet. He is here, I'm certain of it. I must have him. I shall get him guillotined. It will make my fortune."

" Search for him, then ! "

They looked under the chairs and tables, in the cupboards, thrust their pikes under the bed, and probed the mattresses with their bayonets.

Lubin scratched his ear and looked at me slily. Madame de Luzy, dreading that I might be subjected to an embarrassing catechism, said—

" Dear friend, you know the house as well as I do myself. Take the keys and show Monsieur Lubin all over it. I am sure you will be delighted to act as guide to such patriots."

I led them to the cellars, where they turned over the piles of faggots, and drank a fairly large number of bottles of wine ; after which Lubin staved in the full casks with the butt end of his gun, and leaving the cellar flooded with wine, gave the signal of departure. I conducted them out as far as the gate, which I shut on their very heels, and then ran back to let Madame de Luzy know that we were out of danger.

When she heard this, she bent her head over the side of the bed next the wall, and called—

" Monsieur Planchonnet ! Monsieur Planchonnet ! "

A faint sigh was the response.

" God be praised ! " she exclaimed. " Monsieur Planchonnet, you occasioned me the most appalling fear. I thought you were dead."

Then turning towards me—

"My poor friend, you used to take so much delight in declaring, from time to time, that you loved me ; you will never tell me so again ! "

THE BOON OF DEATH BESTOWED

TO ALBERT TOURNIER

THE BOON OF DEATH BESTOWED

WHEN he had for a long while tramped through the deserted streets, André at last went and sat down on the bank of the Seine and watched the water lapping the base of the hill where, in the vanished days of joy and hope, Lucie, his dear mistress, had her home.

For long enough he had not felt so restful.

At eight o'clock he took a bath. Then he strolled into a restaurant in the Palais Royal, and glanced through the newspapers whilst his meal was preparing. In the *Courier of Equality* he read the list of the condemned prisoners who had been executed on the Place de la Révolution on the 24th of Floréal.

He ate his breakfast heartily. Then he rose, looked in a glass to make sure that he was presentably dressed, and that his colour was not likely to betray him, and set out at an easy pace to the other side of the river towards the low house at the corner of the Rue de Seine and the Rue Mazarine. Here were the quarters of Citizen Lardillon, deputy public prosecutor at the revolutionary tribunal, a man well disposed towards André, who had known him first as a capuchin at Angers, and later as a *sans-culotte* in Paris.

He rang, and after an interval of some few minutes, a figure appeared behind a grating commanding the entrance, and Citizen Lardillon, having prudently satisfied himself as to the appearance and name of his visitor, at length threw open the door. His face was broad, his colour high, his eyes glittering, his lips moist, and his ears red. He looked a jovial but worried man. He led André into his ante-chamber.

There, on a small round table, a meal for two was set out. There was a chicken, a pie, a ham, a terrine of foie-gras and various cold meats in aspic. On the floor six bottles were cooling in a pail. A pineapple, cheese of various kinds, and preserved fruits occupied the mantelpiece, and flasks of liqueurs were deposited on a desk littered with papers.

Through the half-open door of the adjoining room a large bed was visible, not yet made.

" Citizen Lardillon," began André, " I have come to beg a favour of you."

" I am quite ready to grant it, citizen, provided it involves no risk to the security of the Republic."

André smilingly replied—

"The service I ask you to do me is not in the least compromising to the safety of either the Republic or yourself."

At a sign from Lardillon, André sat down. "Citizen deputy," he said, "you are aware that for the last two years I have been conspiring against your friends, and that I am the author of the pamphlet entitled, *The Altars of Fear*. You will not be doing me a favour in having me arrested. You will only be doing your duty. Moreover, that is not the service I ask at your hands. But listen: my mistress, to whom I am devoted, is in prison."

Lardillon nodded his head to indicate that he approved of the devotion André confessed to.

"I am sure that you are not unfeeling, Citizen Lardillon. I beg you to procure my reunion with the woman I love, and to have me conveyed to Port Libre as speedily as may be."

"Come, come," said Lardillon, and a smile played upon his lips, which were both delicate and firm, "it is a greater boon than life that you demand of me. You require me to bestow happiness on you, citizen!"

He stretched out the arm nearest to the bedroom, and called—

"Epicharis! Epicharis!"

A big, dark woman entered, her arms and throat still bare, for she had only got as far with her *toilette* as a chemise and petticoat, though a cockade was fastened in her hair.

"Nymph of mine," said Lardillon as he drew her on to his knees, "look upon the face of this citizen, and never forget it! Like us, Epicharis, he is tender-hearted; like us, he realizes that the greatest of ills is to be separated from the beloved one. He wishes to go to prison—ay, to the guillotine—with his mistress, Epicharis. Can I withhold this boon from him?"

"No!" answered the girl, as she tapped the cheeks of the carmagnole-clad monk.

"You are right, my goddess. We shall be earning the gratitude of two devoted lovers. Citizen Germain, give me your address, and this very night you shall sleep in the Bourbe."

"That is agreed?" said André.

"That is agreed," replied Lardillon as he offered him his hand. "Go and find your fair friend, and tell her how you saw Epicharis in Lardillon's embrace. I trust that that recollection may stir your hearts to joyous measures."

André replied that possibly they would be able to call up even more affecting memories, but that he was none the less grateful to Lardillon, and that he only regretted that it was not likely to be in his power to be of service to him in return.

"A humane action needs no recompense," replied Lardillon.

Then he rose, and clasping Epicharis to his heart, said—

"Who knows when our own turn may come?"

> *Omnes eodem cogimur : omnium*
> *Versatur urna ; serius ocius*
> *Sors exitura, et nos in æternum*
> *Exilium impositura cymbæ.*[1]

"In the meanwhile, let us drink! Citizen, will you join us at table?"

Epicharis said it would only be polite of him, and made to seize him by the arm. But he tore himself away, relying on the promise the deputy public prosecutor had made.

---

[1] We all must tread the paths of Fate,
And ever shakes the mortal Urn,
Whose Lot embarks us, soon or late,
On Charon's Boat, ah! never to return.
                              FRANCIS'S *Horace.*

A TALE OF THE MONTH OF
FLORÉAL IN THE YEAR II

TO MADEMOISELLE JEANNE CANTEL

A TALE OF THE MONTH OF FLORÉAL IN THE YEAR II

I

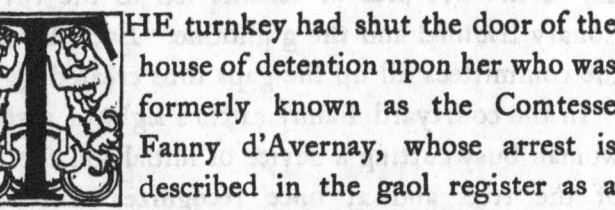

THE turnkey had shut the door of the house of detention upon her who was formerly known as the Comtesse Fanny d'Avernay, whose arrest is described in the gaol register as a step taken "in the interests of public safety," though her actual crime was that she had given shelter to enemies of the Government.

And now she is actually within the venerable edifice in which, once upon a time, the recluses of Port Royal indulged their craving for solitude and community life combined, and out of which it was easy to contrive a prison without making any structural change.

Seated on a bench whilst the registrar enters her name, she thinks—

"Ah, God, why are these things permitted; and what more do You demand of me?"

The turnkey's aspect is rather surly than evil,

and his daughter, who is pretty, looks enchanting in her white cap, with cockade and knot of ribbons in the national colours. By this turnkey Fanny is conducted to a large courtyard, in the middle of which grows a fine acacia. There she will wait till he has prepared a bed and a table for her in a room which already contains five or six prisoners, for the house is crowded. Vainly each day is the overplus of tenants led to the revolutionary tribunal and the guillotine. Each day anew the committees fill up the gaps thus created.

In the courtyard Fanny catches sight of a young woman busy cutting a device of initials on the bark of the tree, and at once recognizes Antoinette d'Auriac, a friend of her childhood.

"What, you here, Antoinette?"

"And you, Fanny? Get them to put your bed by the side of mine. We shall have countless things to tell one another."

"Yes, numbers of things. . . . And Monsieur d'Auriac, Antoinette?"

"My husband? Upon my word, my dear, I had rather forgotten him. It is unfair on my part. To me he has always been irreproachable. . . . I fancy that at the present moment he is in prison somewhere or other."

"And what were you doing just now, Antoinette?"

"Pooh ! . . . What o'clock is it ? If it's five, the friend whose name I was interlacing on the bark there with my own has ceased to exist, for at midday he was haled away to the revolutionary tribunal. His name was Gesrin, and he was a volunteer in the army of the North. I made his acquaintance here in the prison. We passed some agreeable hours together at the foot of this tree. He was a worthy young fellow. . . . But I must set about making you feel at home, my dear."

And seizing Fanny by the waist, she carried her off to the room where she herself slept, and obtained the turnkey's promise not to part her from her friend.

They decided that the following morning they would join forces in washing the floor of their room.

The evening meal, meagrely provided by a patriotic eating-house keeper, was served in common. Each prisoner brought his plate and his wooden cover (metal covers were not allowed), and received his portion of pork and cabbage. At that coarse repast Fanny met women whose gaiety astonished her. As in the case of Madame d'Auriac, their headdresses were scrupulously arranged and they wore unimpeachable costumes. Though death was in sight, they had not lost the womanly desire to please. Their conversation was as gallant as their persons, and Fanny was soon abreast of the love affairs which were knit and unknit in these gloomy courtyards where death lent a keener edge to love. Then, overcome with an indescribable agitation, she was seized with a great longing to clasp another hand in her own.

She called to mind the man who loved her, to whom she had never yielded herself, and a pang of regret, cruel as remorse, rent her heart. Tears as scalding as tears of passion coursed down her cheeks. By the light of the smoky lamp which lit up the table she took note of her companions, whose eyes glittered with fever, and she thought—

"We are condemned to die, all of us. How is it that I am sad and perturbed in spirit, whilst for these women life and death are equally a matter of no concern?"

And all night she wept upon her pallet.

II

TWENTY long monotonous days have passed heavily by. The courtyard where the lovers were wont to go in search of quiet and shade is deserted this evening. Fanny, stifled in the moist air of the corridors, has just sat down on the mound of turf which encircles the base of the old acacia that gives the courtyard its shade. The acacia is in flower, and the breeze passing through its branches emerges charged with the heavy perfume. Fanny catches sight of a scrap of paper fastened to the bark of the tree underneath the device which Antoinette traced there. On this paper she reads some verses by the poet Vigée, like herself a prisoner.

> Here hearts, from taint of treason free,
> Calm victims were of calumny.
> Thanks to the shade outspread above
> They banished grief in dreams of love.
> It heard their sighs and tender fears,
> They oft bedewed it with their tears.

You, whom a time less menacing
Shall to this bare enclosure bring,
Spare yet awhile the kindly tree
Which anguish quelled, and strength upheld,
And half bestowed felicity.[1]

After reading these lines, Fanny relapsed into a thoughtful mood. She mentally reviewed her life, calm and even, her loveless marriage, the state of her own mind, interested in music and poetry, inclined to friendship, sober, untroubled; and then she thought of the love lavished on her by a gallant gentleman, which had wrapped her in its protective folds, yet been accepted unresponsively, as she was better able to realize in the silence of her prison. And, recognizing that she was about to die, she broke down. A sweat of mortal agony rose to her forehead. In her anguish she raised her burning

---

[1] Ici des cœurs exempts de crimes,
Du soupçon, dociles victimes,
Grâce aux rameaux d'un arbre protecteur,
En songeant à l'amour oubliaient leur douleur.
Il fut le confident de leurs tendres alarmes ;
Plus d'une fois il fut baigné de larmes.

Vous, que des temps moins vigoureux
Amèneront dans cette enceinte,
Respectez, protégez cet arbre généreux.
Il consolait la peine, il rassurait la crainte ;
Sous son feuillage on fut heureux.

eyes to the star-strewn sky, and wringing her hands murmured—

"Ah, God, give back to me one little gleam of hope!"

At this moment a light footstep approached. It was Rosine, the turnkey's daughter, coming for a surreptitious talk with her.

"Citizeness," the pretty girl said to her, "to-morrow evening a man who loves you will be waiting on the Avenue de l'Observatoire with a carriage. Take this parcel; it contains clothes like those I am wearing; during supper you will put them on in your bedroom. You are of the same height and fair colouring as myself. In the dusk we might easily be taken one for the other. A warder who is in love with me, and who has engaged in the plot with us, will come up to your room and bring you the basket which I take when I go marketing.

"With him you will descend the staircase (of which he carries a key) leading to my father's lodge. On that side of the prison the outer gate is neither locked nor guarded. You will only have to avoid being seen by my father. My lover will place himself with his shoulder against the little window of the lodge and say, as if he were talking to me: 'Au revoir, Citizeness Rose, and don't be so mischievous!' You will then go quietly

into the street. Whilst this is going on I shall
leave by the main gate, and we shall join one
another in the carriage which is to carry us
away."

As she listened to these words, Fanny drank in
the breath of spring and reawakening nature.
With the whole energy of her being, palpitating
with life, she longed for liberty. She could perceive, could taste the safety that was within her
grasp. And as into the same draught was distilled
an aroma of love, she clasped her hands on her
breast to restrain her happiness. But, little by
little, consideration, a powerful factor in her
character, got the better of sentiment. She
gazed steadily on the turnkey's daughter, and
said—

"Why is it, dear child, that you are prepared
to devote yourself in this way to the interests of
one whom you scarcely know?"

"Oh," replied Rose, this time forgetting to use
the familiar form of speech she had been employ-
ing hitherto, "it's because your kind friend will
give me a large sum of money as soon as you are
free, and then I shall be able to marry Florentin,
my lover. You see, citizeness, that I am working
entirely in my own interests. But I am better
pleased to be the means of rescuing you than one
of the others."

"I thank you for that, my child, but why the preference?"

"Because you are so dainty, and your good friend must be so weary of being separated from you. It is agreed, isn't it?"

Fanny stretched out her hand to take the parcel of clothes Rose was offering her.

But immediately afterwards she drew it back.

"Rose, do you realize that if we are discovered it would mean death to you?"

"Death!" exclaimed the young girl. "You terrify me. Oh, no, I didn't know that!"

Then, as quickly reassured—

"But, citizeness, your kind friend would manage to hide me."

"There isn't a spot in Paris that would prove a safe hiding-place. I thank you for your devotion, Rose; but I can't take advantage of it."

Rose stood as if thunderstruck.

"But you will be guillotined, citizeness, and I shall not be able to marry Florentin!"

"Be easy, Rose. I can do you a service although I can't accept what you offer."

"Oh, no, no! It would be cheating you out of your money."

The turnkey's daughter begged and prayed and wept for long enough. She went on her knees and raised the hem of Fanny's skirt.

T

Fanny gently pushed the girl's hand away and turned her head aside. A moonbeam displayed the peacefulness of the fair face.

It was a lovely night, and a light breeze was moving. The prisoners' tree shook its perfumed branches and scattered its wan flowers upon the head of the voluntary victim.

THE LITTLE LEADEN SOLDIER

TO MADAME GASTON MEYER

THE LITTLE LEADEN SOLDIER

HAT particular night the fever induced by influenza prevented me
from sleeping, and presently I heard
very distinctly three smart taps on
the glass door of a cabinet at the side
of my bed, a cabinet in which I kept in an inextricable medley little figures in Dresden china or
biscuit of Sèvres, terra-cotta statuettes from Tanagra or Myrina, little Renaissance bronzes, Japanese
ivory carvings, Venetian glass, Chinese cups, boxes
in Vernis Martin, lacquer trays, enamel caskets—in
fact, a thousand nothings which a kind of fetish
worship causes one to treasure, and which have the
power of reviving memories of bygone hours,
both gay and melancholy. The taps were faint but
perfectly unmistakable, and by the light of the
nightlight I perceived that they proceeded from a
little leaden soldier installed amid the contents of
the cabinet, who was making efforts to regain his
liberty. He was successful, for soon beneath the
weight of his fist the glazed door swung wide
open. To tell the truth, I was not so surprised as

might be expected. To my mind that little soldier had always worn a suspicious appearance. And during the two years since Madame G. M—— had given him to me, I had been prepared for all sorts of impertinences from him. His uniform is blue turned up with red; he is a *Garde française*, and it is common knowledge that that regiment was not remarkable for discipline.

"Ho, there!" I called out. "What's your name, La Fleur, Brindamour, La Tulipe! can't you make less noise and let me sleep in peace? I am anything but well."

The rascal replied with a growl:

"I haven't changed much, my good man, since I took the Bastille, a hundred years back. On top of that a good many cans of good liquor were emptied. I doubt if many leaden soldiers of my age are still in existence. Good night to you. I am off to parade."

"La Tulipe," I replied with severity, "your regiment was disbanded by order of Louis XVI on the 31st of August, 1789. There is no longer any reason for you to attend parade. Stay where you are in the cabinet!"

La Tulipe twirled his moustache, and then, throwing a sly glance of contempt in my direction, retorted:

"What! do you mean to say you don't know

that every year on the night of the 31st of December, when the children are asleep, our great review takes place, and the leaden soldiers march in procession over the roofs and between the chimneys still joyfully pouring forth the smoke arising from the dying embers of the Yule log? It's a desperate charge, and many a rider takes part in it with never a head on his shoulders. The shades of all the leaden soldiers who have fallen in battle pass by in the rage of combat. Nothing but bent bayonets and broken swords is to be seen. And the spirits of dead dolls, all ashen-faced in the moonbeams, watch them as they go by."

This harangue put me in a quandary.

"Come now, La Tulipe, you mean to say it is a custom, a solemn custom? I have the profoundest respect for all ancient customs and usages, traditions, legends, and popular beliefs. That is what we call folk-lore—a subject we find a great deal of amusement in studying. La Tulipe, it is a great satisfaction to me to learn that you are an observer of tradition. On the other hand, I am not at all sure that I ought to let you leave that cabinet."

"Indeed you ought," said a clear musical voice which I had not heard before, but which I instantly recognized for that of the young woman from Tanagra, who, wrapped in the folds of her himation, occupied a place next to the *Garde française*, on whom she looked down from the graceful dignity of her superior stature. "Indeed you ought. All customs handed down to us by our ancestors are equally worthy of respect. Our fathers knew better than we what is permissible and what forbidden, for they were nearer to the gods. It is only proper, then, to allow this Galatian to perform the warlike rites of his ancestors. In my time they did not wear a ridiculous blue dress turned up with red like our friend here. Their only covering was their buckler. And we held them in great awe. They were barbarians. You yourself are just as much of a Galatian and barbarian. It is all in vain that you have read the poets and historians : you have no true conception of the beauty of life. You were not in the market-place when I used to be spinning wool from Miletus in the courtyard of the house, under the old mulberry tree."

I compelled myself to answer with moderation—

"Lovely Pannychis, your insignificant Greek folk conceived certain forms so beautiful that the eyes and hearts of the judicious will never tire of them. But every day in your market-place such a quantity of drivel was babbled as would give occupation to one of our municipal councils for a whole session. I have no regrets at never having been a citizen of Larissa or Tanagra. At the same time I admit that what you have said is reasonable. It is fitting that customs should be maintained, otherwise they would cease to be customs. Fair Pannychis, who didst spin wool from Miletus under the ancient mulberry tree, not in vain have you assailed my ears with words of good counsel; for on your advice I give La Tulipe permission to go whithersoever folk-lore may call him."

Then a little dairymaid in biscuit of Sèvres, her hands resting on her churn, turned towards me with glances of entreaty.

"Monsieur, do not let him go. He has promised to marry me. He falls in love with every woman he meets. If he goes, I shall never set eyes on him again."

And, hiding her plump cheeks in her apron, she began to weep uncontrollably.

La Tulipe had grown as red as the trimmings of his coat : he could not endure scenes, and he found it extremely distasteful to listen to reproaches which he had richly merited. I reassured my little dairymaid as well as I could, and begged my *Garde française* on no account to loiter about after the review in some Circe's grot. He promised, and I said good-bye to him. But he made no attempt to start. It was extraordinary, but he remained perfectly still on his shelf, as motionless as the dainty trifles surrounding him. I let him perceive my surprise.

"Patience!" he exclaimed. "I cannot set out under your very eyes in that fashion, without infringing every law of the occult world. When you have gone to sleep I shall make off easily enough on a moonbeam, for I am full of expedients. But there is no great hurry, and I can still wait another hour or two. We have nothing better to amuse us than conversation. How would you like me to tell you some tale of days gone by? I know plenty such."

"Yes, tell us one," said Pannychis.

"Tell us one," said the dairymaid.

"Go ahead, then, La Tulipe," said I in my turn.

He sat down, filled his pipe, asked for a glass of beer, coughed, and began his tale with these words :—

THE LEADEN SOLDIER'S STORY

Ninety-nine years ago to the very day, I was standing on a round table with a dozen of my comrades, all of them as like me as if they had been my brothers. Some were standing, some lying down, several had sustained injuries to the head or legs : we were the heroic remnant of a box of leaden soldiers bought the previous year at the fair of Saint Germain. The room was hung with pale blue silk. It contained a spinet with the Prayer from Orpheus open upon it, a few chairs with lyre-shaped backs, a lady's escritoire of mahogany, a white bed decked with roses ; and all along the cornice were perched pairs of doves. Everything combined to convey an impression of affecting charm. The lamp diffused its soft light, and the flame on the hearth quivered like wings beating in the dusk. Clad in a dressing-gown, and seated in front of her escritoire, her delicate neck bending beneath the circling masses of her magnificent fair hair, Julie was turning over the letters tied up with ribbons, which had lain hidden in the drawers of the bureau.

Midnight strikes ; the outward sign of the imaginary leap from one year to another. The dainty timepiece, on which is poised a laughing, golden Cupid, proclaims that the year 1793 has come to an end.

Just as the hands of the clock meet, a small phantom figure makes its appearance. Through a door which stands half open, a pretty child has crept out of the dressing-room, where he has his bed, and run in his nightshirt to fling himself into his mother's arms and wish her a happy new year.

"A happy new year, Pierre ? . . . Ah! thank you, thank you ! But do you know what a happy year is ? "

He thought he did ; but, all the same, she wished to make quite sure that he knew.

"A year is happy, my darling, when it passes on its way bringing us neither hatreds nor fears."

She embraces him ; then she carries him back to the bed he has escaped from, and then returns to her seat in front of the escritoire. She glances first at the flames leaping on the hearth, and then at the letters from which dried flowers are falling. It is heartrending to have to burn them. Yet it must be done. For these letters, if they were discovered, would consign to the guillotine both him who wrote them and her who received them. If it was only herself that was in danger, she would not burn them, so weary is she of her contest for life with the executioners. But she thinks of him, proscribed, denounced, pursued, hidden away in some garret at the other end of Paris. A single one of these letters would be enough to put his pursuers on his track and deliver him over to death.

Pierre is sleeping snugly in the neighbouring dressing-room ; the cook and Nanon have gone to their rooms in the upper regions. The intense silence of a snow-clad town reigns all around. The keen, clear air brightens the flame on the hearth. Julie has made up her mind to burn these letters, and it is a task she cannot carry out—how well she knows it!—without recalling events of the profoundest sadness. She will burn the letters, but not until she has read them through once again.

The letters are all arranged in succession, for Julie imparts to everything around her a measure of the orderliness which is natural to her.

These, already growing yellow, date from three years ago, and in the silence of the night Julie lives over again the magic hours. Not a single page is surrendered to the flames until she has conned it over at least ten times, syllable by treasured syllable.

The stillness all around her is unbroken. From time to time she goes to the window, raises the curtain, glances through the oppressive gloom at the tower of Saint Germain des Prés silvered by the moon, and then resumes her slow labours of pious destruction. Why should she not for the last time rejoice over these delicious pages? Why deliver to the flames these cherished lines ere she has for ever imprinted them on her heart. Stillness prevails everywhere, and her spirit leaps with youth and love.

She reads—

"Though absent, I behold you, Julie. I go on my way, surrounded by images which my mind conjures up. I behold you, not cold and unnerved,

but alive, animated, ever changing, yet ever perfect.
Around you in my dreams I gather the most
gorgeous spectacles the world can yield. How
happy is Julie's lover! He finds charms in all
things, since in all things he finds her. In loving
her it is life he loves; he marvels at this world
which she irradiates; he treasures this earth which
she adorns. Love unveils to him the hidden
mystery of things. He apprehends the infinite
forms of creation; they all display to him symbols
of Julie; he hears the unnumbered voices of
nature; they all murmur in his ear the name of
Julie. He plunges his gaze rapturously into the
inmost heart of the daylight, with the thought that
that fortunate light bathes also the countenance of
Julie, and casts as it were a divine caress on the
loveliest of human forms. This evening the earliest
stars will thrill his being; he will say: 'Perhaps
at this very moment she too is gazing on them.'
He inhales her in all the odours borne on the air.
He desires to kiss the very ground she treads
on. . . .

"My Julie, if I am fated to fall beneath the axe
of the persecutor, and like Algernon Sidney to die
for liberty, death itself will be unable to restrain
my indignant ghost in the land of shades which
holds not you. I shall fly to you, my beloved.
Often will my spirit return to hover around you."

She reads and dreams. Night is coming to a close. Already a pallid light pierces the curtains : it is morning. The servants have begun their work. She must finish her own. Has she caught the sound of voices ? No ; all around her is silence, still. . . .

Yes, all around is silence, for the snow deadens the tramp of feet. They are coming ; they halt outside. Blows fall heavily on the door.

She has not time to hide the letters, to close the escritoire. All she can do she does ; she takes the papers in armfuls and throws them underneath the sofa, the valance of which touches the floor ; a few letters are scattered on the carpet ; she pushes them under with her foot, seizes a book, and flings herself into a chair.

The president of the district enters, followed by a dozen of his pikemen. He is an elderly chaircaner named Brochet, who shivers with ague, and whose bloodshot eyes roam in an unspeakably loathsome fashion.

He makes a sign to his men to keep guard over the approaches, and then turning to Julie, announces—

"We have just received information, citizeness, that you are in correspondence with the agents of Pitt, and with emigrés and conspirators in the prisons. In the name of the law, I am here to take possession of your papers. It is now some time since you were pointed out to me as an aristocrat of the most dangerous type. Citizen Rapoix, whom you see before you" (here he indicated one of his followers), " has confessed that in the severe winter of 1789, you gave him both money and clothes with a view to corrupting him. Magistrates of a timid tendency and wanting in patriotism have shown you leniency over long. But I am master now, in my turn, and you shall not escape the guillotine. Deliver up your papers, citizeness ! "

" Take them yourself," said Julie ; " my escritoire is unlocked."

There still remained in the drawers certain certificates of births, marriages, and deaths, tradesmen's bills, and title-deeds, which one by one Brochet examined. He fumbled with them, and laid them aside with the suspicious air of a man who reads but poorly, and from time to time exclaimed : " Scandalous ! The name of the so-called king is not effaced. Scandalous, scandalous, I call it ! "

From his manner Julie concludes that his visit will be lengthy and scrupulous. She cannot resist taking a furtive glance at the side of the sofa, and she sees at once the corner of a letter peeping out from under the valance like the white ear of a cat. At this sight her agony vanishes suddenly. The certainty that she is lost brings back to her a quiet assurance, and her face takes on a calm indistinguishable from an expression of complete security. She has no doubt that the men will observe this scrap of paper so patent to her own eyes. Its whiteness on the red carpet positively screams at her. But she cannot guess whether they will discover it at once or whether some time must first elapse. This doubt occupies and distracts her mind. At this tragic moment she indulges in a sort of joke with herself as she watches the patriots moving further away from or nearer to the sofa.

Brochet, who has finished with the papers in the escritoire, becomes impatient, and declares that he will certainly find what he has come in search of.

He overthrows the furniture, turns the pictures round, and raps the panelling with the pommel of his sword to detect hiding-places. He can discover nothing. He smashes a panel of looking-glass to see if anything is concealed behind it. There is nothing.

Whilst this is going on his men raise some of the squares of parquet. They declare with oaths that a beggarly aristocrat is not going to have the laugh of honest *sans-culottes*. But never one of them espies the little white wisp which peeps from under the valance of the sofa.

U

They march Julie into the other rooms of the suite and demand all her keys. They burst open the cupboards, shiver the windows to splinters, smash up the chairs, drag the stuffing from the upholstery. And they find nothing.

Still Brochet is not yet despondent; he returns to the bedroom.

"In God's name! the papers are here; I'm certain of it!"

He examines the sofa, declares that it has a suspicious appearance, probes it five or six times with his sword from end to end. Still he finds no traces of what he seeks, utters a horrible oath, and gives his men orders to depart.

He is already at the door, when, returning a step or two towards Julie, he raises his fist and shouts—

"Live in dread of my return! I am the sovereign people!"

And he goes out, last of all.

At length all are gone. She hears the clatter of their tread grow fainter on the staircase. She is saved! Her imprudence has not betrayed him— him whom she loves! She runs, with a jubilant little laugh, to embrace the tiny Pierre, who is sleeping with his fists clenched, just as though everything round his cradle had not been turned upside down.

When he had finished his tale, La Tulipe re-lighted his pipe, which had gone out, and emptied his glass.

"My friend," I said, "justice is a virtue. For a *Garde française* it must be admitted that you are a finished story-teller. But I have a strong impression that I have already heard that story somewhere."

"It may be that Julie herself related it. She was a creature of infinite wit."

"And what became of her?"

"She knew some happy times in the days of the Consulate. Nevertheless, of an evening she would whisper sorrowful secrets to the trees in her park. You see, Monsieur, she was better armed against death than against love."

"And he who wrote such elegant letters?"

"He became a baron and prefect under the Empire."

"And little Pierre?"

"He died a colonel of *gendarmerie*, at Versailles, in 1859."

"The deuce he did!"